# A Port in Pieces

## A PORT CITY HIGH NOVEL

# SHANNON FREEMAN

SADDLEBACK
EDUCATIONAL PUBLISHING

High School High

Taken

Deported

The Public Eye

The Accident

Listed

Traumatized

*A Port in Pieces*

www.sdlback.com

ISBN-13: 978-1-62250-775-7
ISBN-10: 1-62250-775-4
eBook: 978-1-61247-986-6

Printed in Malaysia

20 19 18 17 16   3 4 5 6 7

## ACKNOWLEDGMENTS

First, I give honor to God because he gave me a story that needed to be told. Without him, there would be no Port City High. Thank you for giving me the fortitude to make it to the end.

To the readers of Port City High, if you have made it this far with me, thank you. If it wasn't for you, then there would be no need for me. Hopefully, this final book sums everything up and doesn't disappoint. Don't forget, there's a story locked in each of us dying to get out. Thanks again!

To Saddleback Educational Publishing, thank you for making me a part of your vision. It's been a dream come true. I can't believe that this is the end of Port City High! Thank God you had a new vision for me. You asked me to step outside my comfort zone and write a middle school series. Of all of the writers you have on your team, you chose me. It is an honor to continue this journey with you. Thanks again.

I have a large family, but there are those of you that I have to mention who continually support me. Seeing your faces at book signings and receiving your accolades makes me feel at home in a crowded room. Thank you for your support: Debbie, Dallas, Louis, Stephanie, Jean, Midge, Crystal, Rayetta, Googie, Betty Jo, Billie, Norma Jean, Lisa, Carolyn, Dawn, Machelle, Shanell, Kelli, Lil Louis, Diamond, Jessie, Kenetia, Marcus, and Marcie.

In regards to my friends old and new, you have truly blessed me with your support. Thank you so much! Fe, Woods, Dez, Ne, Qiana, Kenya, Joy, Evette,

Diasheena, Tia, Jenn, Angel, Kayla, Shermette, Adrienne, Latania, Shaq, Daniel, Hope, Henry, Mr. Wagner, Roy, Danielle, Vinnie, Myrna, Craig, Sharon, Sasha, NiDeja, Ms. Ida, Chavon, Karesse, and last and but far from least, Mr. Dunnie ... thank you for everything.

For my mom and sister, Mom always reminded us that we are all we have in this world and to keep each other first. Even though our family has grown, the foundation that was set all those years ago is what keeps us as close as we are. Both of you support me the way that only a mother and sister can. Your love means more to me than words can say. Thank you for your encouragement and for always believing in me. I love you both.

Thank you to Kaymon, Kingston, Addyson, and Brance. Just being here makes your father and me that much happier. You are our blessing. I love each one of you.

Finally, I'm going to end the way that I started. My soul mate, my life partner, my best friend, my everything ... Derrick Freeman, I love you. People don't understand how we have time in a day to do what we do. Sometimes I don't either, but we make it happen. Thank you for being understanding, giving, and loving. You always know what I need.

I know this was longer than usual, but it's the finale! Hope you enjoy!

# Prologue

There was a lot to do since Hurricane Adam had blown through Port City. The billion dollars in damage still left its mark around the small town. Trees that had been thrown like little twigs over the streets had now been cleared. But the streetlights and traffic signals now sitting at the bottom of the Gulf of Mexico had not been replaced.

The temporary stop signs marking intersections were a reminder of what the people along the port had endured, and how far they had to go to be whole again.

It was the same at Port City High School. Even though the money had been raised to get students back into their beloved school, only the essentials had been fixed. None of the other damage could be repaired until recovery money was in the hands of the school district.

A special team assembled. Their job was to clear the school of debris and garbage. Once that job was complete, contractors, parents, and student volunteers were allowed to begin painting. Portions of the school were now ready for business.

"We did it," Shane said, standing in the foyer of Port City High.

"I'm proud of you girls," Trent said, standing next to Marisa. "This could not have happened if the three of you hadn't stepped in."

"Love, it couldn't have happened if people like you didn't come home for the holidays and help us out. Thank you so much for staying," Marisa said, looking adoringly at her boyfriend.

"Anything for you. Let's go check the lobby again."

"Ew, go back to Arkansas already. You two are gross," Shane said, making faces at her friends. "See y'all later."

Trent and Marisa left, heading down the hall.

"You want me to show you a little love," Ashton said, winking at her.

"Fool, no. We're gonna inspect our work."

Brandi and Erick Wright were trying to move paint and supplies into one of the classrooms that was turned into a temporary storage room. "Ashton, grab the other side of this plank," Shane said, jumping in to help them remove some of the materials. Once they were done clearing the hallway, they all sat on the floor, propped against a wall.

"Mrs. Montgomery is supposed to be

coming soon. When are you going back to school, E?" Shane asked Erick.

"I have a few more days in town. After this, I need a nap or two before I have to jump back into my spring schedule. The University of Texas is brutal. They are trying to break everybody. They like to weed through the freshman class."

"Fun," Brandi said, getting a glimpse of what campus life could be like for her.

"Bran, come on. You love a challenge," Shane told her.

"I'm just happy we won't be a part of all that freshman craziness. We will be right here at Port City College, getting through basic courses, easy breezy," Brandi said.

Shane laughed. "True. I'm not into torture. I just want to do my four years, get my degree, and be out." Shane smiled, picturing the three of them in the same classes.

"Are you really staying in Port City

another year, Shane? I would have thought you'd be out of here on the next train," Ashton chimed in.

Before anyone could respond, Trent and Marisa walked up with Mrs. Montgomery. A crowd of volunteers followed her. The principal looked different in a pair of skinny jeans and Ugg boots. She was usually in a suit and heels, with a simple string of pearls. She spoke to the cleanup crew.

"I can't say thank you enough. This school looks amazing in comparison to just a few weeks ago. I really didn't think this was possible until some people talked me into it. You can thank Shane, Brandi, and Marisa. Without them, we might still be at Riverdale." The group began to clap and cheer. "Now, there's nothing else we can do before the beginning of the semester tomorrow. Burgers on me. To Jerry's!" Mrs. Montgomery declared.

The girls turned back to look at the school before getting into their cars. "This is it," Brandi said.

"Last semester," Marisa added.

"Senior year," Shane concluded. "Welcome home."

# CHAPTER 1

# Shane

Shane sat working at her computer until her eyes began to cross. Editing pictures was one thing, but editing a documentary was entirely different. There was a learning curve that Shane was not accustomed to. It seemed as though she was constantly consulting the Internet to learn new techniques. Her documentary video of life in Port City just before and right after Hurricane Adam was nearly complete. She was feeling more confident in her skills.

She closed her laptop and went downstairs to have dinner with her family.

"Shane, go back upstairs and change your clothes," her mother told her as soon as she walked into the dining room. Their good plates were already on the table, and her mother looked as though she were preparing for the president's arrival.

"Why?"

"Because we are having company tonight. Now go."

"I don't care about company. I've been working too hard on *The Blues* to care about what anybody thinks about my appearance. Can I just eat in my room? I'm really not in the mood for all this."

"This is very important. Your dad is doing everything he can in order to get this city back up and running. One of those things is to get this supplier to assist us. Mister Betancourt is supposed to have connections. It would probably be great for your documentary too. You never know what you could learn from him."

"Okay, okay. I'll go change." She

grabbed a strawberry and dipped it in the chocolate fountain that her mother loved to use when they had guests over.

"Not another bite, little girl. Now go change."

Shane kissed her mom on the cheek and ran to change clothes. She knocked on Robin's door. She heard her nephew, Aiden, wreaking havoc. "Hey, you know we have company coming for dinner?" Shane asked Robin.

"My fiancé is on his way to pick us up."

"You do know that I know Gavin, right? You don't have to call him your fiancé."

"I like saying it, though. It sounds good. Wanna see my ring?" she asked, extending her hand and showing off her rock.

Shane picked Aiden up and swung him around. "Yo mama is cuckoo for Cocoa Puffs. Yes, she is, but that's okay 'cause you have Auntie."

"Don't tell my baby that I'm cuckoo."

"If the word fits." She laughed, walking

out of her sister's room, trying to close the door without Aiden following. It was impossible. The boy loved his auntie Shane. They were kindred spirits.

When back in her room, she located the most comfortable, yet acceptable, dressy outfit she could find: skinny jeans, a flannel shirt, and a statement necklace. Simple and cute. She brushed her hair and added hairspray to fight the unruly strands that seemed to always scream for attention. She added light pink blush to her cheeks and lip gloss to her lips. Perfection.

Their guest had dark skin and a Caribbean island accent. He told them his family had come from Haiti, and that he had once lived in New York City. He now resided in Miami.

"That's a lot of moving around, Mister Betancourt. So you aren't married?" Mrs. Foster asked him curiously.

"Uh, no. Marriage is not for me. I enjoy the single life."

During dessert, Shane decided it was time to quiz their guest for information. "I'm filming a documentary about Hurricane Adam," Shane shared with Mr. Betancourt. "Can I ask you a question?"

"Sure," he responded, clearing his throat.

"Which city was hit the worst? Which hurricane did the most damage?"

"It's funny you should ask that. It seems to me that once those hurricanes pass, each area looks the same: destroyed. But you were lucky in Port City. I know it doesn't feel like it right now, but I believe that with the proper builder, you can be up and running by the summertime. You can put this whole thing behind you. Like it never happened."

"Well, that's what I wanted to talk to you about, Mr. Betancourt," Mr. Foster admitted. "We need supplies, and we need a lot of them. Sheetrock. Shingles. Wood."

"You have come to the right place,

Mister Foster. I have connections and resources. However, I am not a builder."

"Let's talk in my office, Mister Betancourt. I have some ideas that I wanted to share with you."

When they retreated to her father's office, Shane helped her mother clear away the dinner dishes. "I'm so happy Dad found this guy. The school has a long way to go, but these blue roofs are killing me. I hate seeing Port City this way."

"You are your father's child. You ever thought about going into politics too, Shane?"

"Not for me, Mom. I'm a free spirit, and there's no freedom in politics. You have to fit into their little box, or you are front-page news. No, I'm cool behind the camera. It's where I belong."

Her mother laughed. "You can't be sure what you want to do this early in life, Shane. Explore your options when you get to college. You never know. The world could open up for you."

"Mom, I know what I want to do. The camera is like air for me. I need it." She kissed her mom and ran upstairs to her room. She had to get back to work. The long dinner with their guest had set her back on her goal for the evening.

# CHAPTER 2

# Marisa

Sitting comfortably by the cozy fireplace at Trent's house was a familiar feeling for Marisa. She could hear his mom in the kitchen making hot chocolate and cookies. She had offered to help, but Mrs. Walker would hear none of it. "You go enjoy some time with Trent. He'll be leaving soon."

"You know I enjoy helping you in the kitchen, Mrs. Walker."

"Marisa, you are always welcome here, even when Trent's back in Arkansas. You need to ride out there with us for one of his games."

Marisa's eyes glazed over. She thought about her junior year when the girl he was dating answered his dorm room phone. Showing up in Arkansas sounded like a setup for disaster. She would hate to accidentally meet one of those girls who fawned all over Trent.

"Hey," Mrs. Walker said, trying to snap her back to reality, "he loves you, Marisa. After all, how many people can say that they have a daughter-in-law who is a top model?"

Marisa laughed at the absurdity of the statement. "Number one, I'm no top model. Number two, daughter-in-law?"

"What are you two in here babbling about?"

"Nothing, you guys go start that fire, Trent. Enjoy the little time you have together." Mrs. Walker winked at Marisa as Trent led her to the family room. There he added the logs to the fireplace and began working to build a fire for them.

"I'm glad we aren't on *Survivor*. You may want to get help from your dad." Marisa couldn't help but tease him. They both had a healthy sense of humor and loved to laugh at themselves.

"Woman, I builds my own fire." And like magic, a tiny flame began, and he worked on it until it grew healthily.

"Nice job, my king," she said, cuddling him in her arms as he joined her on the couch. "So how much longer do we have?"

"Shhh, don't talk about it."

"Just tell me."

"No. Did you apply to the YOU of A yet?"

She studied her hands. "I have not. I'm staying in Port City, Trent. I told you that. We made a pact."

"Come on, Marisa. Are you always going to choose them over me?"

"Trent—" He hushed her with a kiss.

"I just want you to think about it. That's all," he said, leaning his forehead against hers. She nodded in agreement, but the decision was already made. She was staying in Port City for one more year with Shane and Brandi. Freshman year of community college, and then they could separate.

"Cookies are ready," Mrs. Walker said, interrupting their moment with a tray of cookies and hot chocolate.

"You are a hard act to follow," Marisa said as she studied the tray of homemade oatmeal, chocolate chip, and peanut butter cookies.

"I'm sure you'll do just fine," his mother said. "Trent, I hope you're packed. We have to be on the road at five. Coach called and said that your practices are starting back up immediately."

"Tomorrow?" Marisa asked, looking from Trent to his mom. His mother sensed that she had said the wrong thing and left them alone. "Tomorrow? When were you going to tell me, Trent?"

"I didn't want tonight to be about that. I just wanted to enjoy you and call you from the road."

"That's not fair. *Estúpido!* That was your big plan?" She popped him on the side of the head and went to the bathroom to compose herself. *It's happening all over again.* She splashed water on her face. "What a stupid girl," she said to her reflection. She left the bathroom to tell the Walkers good-bye.

"Mari, you're not going to say good-bye to me. You're overreacting. Come on, don't leave like this," he pleaded with her.

"I don't trust you, Trent. Every little thing is huge, and it's not healthy. I'm not going to YOU of A. It's time for the both of us to move on."

"Marisa." He tried to stop her from walking outside. "Come on, Mari. What we have is—"

"Over. I'm sorry, Trent, but I can't let you hurt me again. And you just did."

"I was just trying to enjoy our last night together. I was—"

She kissed him and walked out the door. She knew she had overreacted. Everything inside her was screaming, "Go back and say you're sorry! Go. Go." But she couldn't. She didn't want him to leave. She didn't want to be alone. She loved him too much to think of him cozying up to some college girl tomorrow after leaving her arms tonight. She shook her head to get the image out, but it was already there.

Ever since last year, she couldn't completely trust him. She didn't want to go back to that place of hurt. It had caused too much pain. She had started partying and drinking, and then there was the accident. The accident had changed everything. It took Bethany's life. No, she couldn't go back, so it was time to just let go. To let Trent go.

By the time she got home, she was all cried out. Her face and eyes were red and puffy. She looked like a nightmare. As soon as she walked through the door, her mother was calling her, "*Mi hija, estamos en la cocina.*"

"*Qué paso*, Mama?" She saw her father as the words escaped her lips. "*Dios mio*! Papa! What are you doing home?"

"I have a meeting in the morning with Mister Foster and some supplier. He's supposed to be the man who can really help me kick off my relaunched construction business, *Mi Casa es Su Casa.*"

"Catchy, Papa. Whatever, whoever, I'm just glad to see your face. How long will you be here?"

"Well, it depends on how this meeting goes. I really don't know yet. I told them that I had to be back to work on Monday for sure."

"Awesome!" She kissed her father and

ran to her room. She had a lot to digest. Her parents hadn't noticed her tear-stained cheeks or puffy eyes. She didn't want to talk about it. She welcomed her father home and left as quickly as she could. Trent, her father, school starting back up ... her emotions were all over the place. She needed to find her center.

# CHAPTER 3

# Brandi

"Hey, B, I'm outside. What you got up for the night?"

"Dub, you can't just show up at my house. I'm not even home."

"Dang, girl, I just wanted to chill with you tonight. Where you at? I'm coming to get you."

It was Erick's last night in town before returning to UT, and Brandi wanted to do something special. Shane told her what a wonderful time she had on her date with Ryan Petry her sophomore year, when he took her to the museum. Erick was into that kind of thing, so she surprised him with the date.

They had gone through a new exhibit highlighting the rich history of Port City. There were so many artists, musicians, writers, and athletes who were celebrated there. It was eye-opening how much talent had been birthed in one small Texas town. It made them want more. They shared a moment in that museum that opened their eyes to the world. There was so much more beyond Port City.

Now here she sat waiting for Erick to come back with their evening's snacks, and enjoying the ambience of the quaint little food carts strewn with twinkling lights. It was just as Shane had described the museum's courtyard: perfect. The January chill swept through, but with heat lamps, a down jacket, and warm boots, she was just fine. The only thing ruining her evening was Dub. She knew she should have never answered her phone.

"Dub, I can't—"

"Hot chocolate, my queen," Erick said, setting her cup in front of her.

"Oh, that's why you can't chill wit yo boy, cuz you out wit dat white dude. Man! Bye, B!" he yelled into the phone. She politely put her phone back on the table facedown. The last thing she was going to allow Dub to do was ruin this moment with Erick.

"Who was that?"

"Nobody," she said matter-of-factly. "Now, as for you, stop asking me to come to UT this year. Austin is going to have to wait. I'm staying here. You know that."

"Okay, but you can't blame me for trying. I miss you when I'm there."

"Boy, stop. Those college girls are keeping you busy, I'm sure. I like what we have, Erick, an awesome friendship." They were attracted to each other. There was no denying that, but they never ventured past the friendship stage.

"Aren't you even a little bit curious to see what would happen if we were more than friends? Just a little curious?"

She felt warm all over despite the fact that it was freezing cold outside. The more time she spent with Erick, the more she liked him. "E, listen ... you know what I've been through. I'm guarded."

"Girl, this is the changing of the guard, and I'm in charge. You'll see."

His confidence was attractive. Cocky, but not an egomaniac. Sensitive, but not wishy-washy. It's what made him so extremely sexy, and what allowed Brandi to be connected to him in a way that she wasn't connected to anybody else. Erick Wright. Who would have thought they would be here together.

They met on the debate team. And she had been so rude to him. But he never returned her rudeness. He was always a nice guy. Their awkward first meeting was long forgotten. They realized that they enjoyed each other's company. Plus, he was the sexiest white boy she had ever seen, and his swag was on point.

Shoot, Erick was really the sexiest guy of any ethnicity that she had come across, and he knew how to treat her. She was almost tempted to go to UT with him in the fall. She had already been accepted with a full ride, but she asked the recruiter to hold it for one year so that she could get her house in order.

Brandi knew that once she separated from Marisa and Shane, they would never live in the same city again. She just knew it, and she wasn't ready. No, she was making the right decision. Her girls had always been there for her. She wasn't about to start choosing a guy over them—not now, not ever.

# CHAPTER 4

# College Confusion

"Attention, all seniors," the familiar voice of the principal's secretary resonated over the intercom. She had the most distinctive voice, a little raspy Southern drawl. Mrs. Hunter's voice was one that they would always remember. "Attention, all seniors. There will be a mandatory meeting in the auditorium during sixth period. Teachers, please accompany any seniors in your class to the auditorium during their sixth period class. Thank you."

"What now?" Shane said to Marisa and Brandi as they ate their lunch.

"We all have full scholarships to the college of our choice," Brandi said, speaking in a dreamy voice.

"And then you woke up. So, any word on your parents letting you stay in the dorms this fall?" Marisa asked her friends.

"I don't know about that. Port City College had more damage than PCH. The students who go to college there had to move out of their dorms. They probably won't be ready," Shane told her friends.

"That really does suck," Brandi interjected as the bell began to ring. "Are y'all sure that we are making the right decision staying here?"

"I'm sure," Shane said. "It's just one year."

A small smile crept to Marisa's face. "One more year. I'm going to cry so hard when we go our separate ways. I can't even think about it."

"Me too," Shane and Brandi said in unison.

"Find me during sixth period so we can sit together," Marisa said, emptying into the crowded hallway with the other PCH students frantically trying to make it to fourth period on time.

By the time sixth period arrived, the seniors were all anxiously anticipating the meeting. What was it about? They piled into the auditorium noisily as the principal and assistant principal tried to quiet them down. But it was their last semester of high school and turning down wasn't an option.

As Brandi walked in, she saw Shane and Marisa waving her over. She joined her two besties just as the assembly was getting ready to start. Mrs. Montgomery was already at the microphone. She waited as each student found a seat. "Teachers, if you are close to students who are still standing, please get them into a seat as quickly and quietly as possible. We have a lot to cover today." *A lot to cover? What is this about?* The whispering in the audience grew in intensity as they all pondered the nature of the meeting.

"Okay. Welcome, seniors!" she yelled, and it sent them all into a frenzy.

They began to cheer loudly and chant "Seniors! Seniors!"

Mrs. Montgomery continued. "Well, seniors, we have some housecleaning to do today."

"This is not going to be good," Shane whispered.

"Um-hm," Brandi agreed with her.

"I'm going to rip the Band-Aid off this afternoon. There's no other way to do it. Port City College will not open its doors for classes for the fall semester. The repairs will begin during the summer and will not be ready by the time school begins."

Hands raised across the auditorium as her words began to sink in. "Please hold all of your questions until I'm done speaking. Hope is not lost, so don't panic. We have reached out to Baymont College, and they are more than willing to transfer those of you who were already accepted at PCC," she said. "Also, I have a list of colleges that have granted us emergency enrollment due to the current condition of our city."

"What are we going to do now?" Marisa asked her friends, who seemed to be searching for answers too.

"We go to Baymont," Brandi said. She pictured her sister's face. She had already promised her that she would stay home for one more year. She couldn't bear to tell her those plans had changed.

"Baymont? I don't want to go there," Marisa told them.

"I don't either," Shane said. She quickly raised her hand. Mrs. Montgomery called on her, and Mrs. Hunter brought her the microphone. "Mrs. Montgomery, what if we want to attend a college that's not on the emergency enrollment list? What do we do then?"

"Talk to my secretary or your counselor, and we will make sure you are taken care of. Don't worry. Everyone in the country knows what we are going through. They have been welcoming our students with open arms—if your grades and test scores are good enough. So please, everyone, remain calm."

Many of the students weren't fazed at all because they never planned to attend PCC. The ones who were already accepted and had decided to stay home for college seemed rocked to the core. Tears were shed, friends were consoled, and new plans were being made all over the auditorium.

"Well, girls, back to the drawing board," Shane said to them.

"Are we still going to stay together?" Marisa asked them.

Brandi nodded in agreement. "Definitely. As long as they will hold my scholarship at UT, I'm good."

"Well, we have to come up with a plan because before we know it, graduation will be here."

"I know," Marisa said, looking like a deer caught in headlights. They left the auditorium and went their separate ways. They each needed time to think.

# CHAPTER 5

# Marisa

The Maldonado family sat in Pappasito's, enjoying a wonderful evening out. They were celebrating, and it felt good. Not only had the business connection Mr. Maldonado made worked out, but he was able to quit his job in San Antonio a lot sooner than he thought. He officially ended his employment, and this had been his first full day back at home with his family.

Mrs. Maldonado leaned over and kissed her husband gently on the cheek. "It's so nice having you home, George. I don't know what we did to deserve this, but I feel so blessed."

"Mom, can you please not kiss? It's so gross, and people are watching us," Isi complained.

"Mi hija, nobody is watching, and I don't care if they are."

When their food arrived, Marisa laughed out loud. "Mom, you could have made all of this at home," Marisa said.

"Yes, Mari, but I didn't have to. Isn't that wonderful? Your mother needs a break sometimes too."

She was right. She took care of everybody in that house. If there was a need, Lupe Maldonado jumped right in to fill it. She was a great mother.

"So, Marisa, have you decided what you are going to do next year? We have to make some quick decisions," her mother warned her.

"I've been working with the counselor. I sent out four applications, and each school has extended the deadline for me. If all else fails, I can just go to Baymont. It won't be the end of the world."

"Yes it would," Nadia joined in. She was studious and had aspirations that reached way beyond Baymont College. "Go as far as you can and see as much as you can. Don't go to Baymont. You are too big for that. You're a supermodel, for God's sake."

"I am not a supermodel, Nadia, but thanks. Sometimes you do what you have to do. You'll see what I mean. It's just life."

She surprised herself giving life advice. The closer she came to graduation, the more mature she became. It was as if she was turning some makeshift corner.

"What your sister is telling you is true, Nadia. Look at how much we've had to adjust in this family. You take the good with the bad, and work with what you have."

"Well, that's not happening to me.

I already know where I'm going for my undergrad."

Her sister detailed her entire future for them, and they learned a bit more about her than they had known before. It was the wonderful thing about going out to eat together; they were able to enjoy each other instead of running around the kitchen.

"And what about you, mi hijo?" Mr. Maldonado asked his son.

Romero shrugged his shoulders. "I don't know. I guess I'll come work with you, Papa."

"Well, we will see about that, Rom. Make sure you have a plan, though."

They continued to eat their food, but Isi wasn't happy. "Nobody asked what I want to do."

"What do you want to do?" Marisa asked, putting down her fork and giving Isi her complete attention.

"I'm going to be an actress. I can't wait.

I'm going to be a huge star one day." They laughed at her ambition, but at the same time, they knew she could do it if she wanted to. "You'll see," Isi said.

By the time Marisa got home, she had two voice mails from Trent. She had intentionally left her phone at home so that she could spend some quiet time with her family. She knew her cell phone would not allow her to do that. She picked up the phone and called him back.

"Did you fill out that application yet?"

"Is that how you answer the phone, Trent? And yes, I filled it out, but I'm still not coming to Arkansas."

"Marisa, talk to me. You can't hide behind Shane and Brandi any longer. PCC is not opening. Y'all have to separate anyway, so what's the real reason you're not coming?"

"Look, this is your sophomore year in college. You'll be a junior by the time I get there. Do you think I want to be in

Arkansas by myself? You left me in Port City, but this is home. Do you really want me to go through that drama again? Come on, Trent."

"You'll just transfer to wherever I'm playing basketball. You know you want to live as a basketball player's girlfriend while you are in college."

"No, I really don't want to be with some cheating, gone all the time—"

"Whoa, why all athletes gotta cheat?"

"Not all athletes. You! Must I remind you?"

"You don't have to. It's been the same thing since I left. I'm tired of fighting, Marisa. I've apologized a million times. You have to stop living in the past."

"Dude, you are right. This whole conversation is about me living in the past. I'm tired of this roller coaster ride, Trent."

"You're the one on the roller coaster. I know what *I* want. It's because you can't get over one little mistake."

"I caught you once, but that doesn't mean it was your only mistake. You know what? This doesn't even matter. I have to go, Trent. I have to think about me and my future."

"Marisa! Marisa!"

She ended the call. Their relationship was awful. They were either way up or way down, and this college conversation seemed to always end badly. She hated it, but she needed space to think about herself for a change—not Trent, not Shane, not Brandi—just plain old Marisa.

## CHAPTER 6

# Brandi

$\mathcal{G}$et the pots out of the closet, Bran. The roof is leaking again," her mother complained. She turned to her husband, exasperated. "Please call George. He has to come and fix this."

Mr. Haywood had been trying not to bother Mr. Maldonado. He had already complained to him about the problems they were having with the roof. Mr. Maldonado's workers had completed the temporary patch job. However, there was water pouring into their home.

Mr. Maldonado had sworn that when

the supplies came in, the Haywoods would be first on the to-do list. That still did not make them feel any better on a night like this when it seemed as though the heavens had opened up.

Brandi could tell that her dad was uncomfortable when he called Mr. Maldonado. It made Brandi uncomfortable to listen. She had no problem calling anyone and making them stand by the work they had done. *I guess I get that from my mom,* she thought as she walked out of the room. "You better talk to Mr. Maldonado yourself, Mom. If you let Daddy handle it, we'll have pots in our living room until next year."

Her mother sighed. Then she got up and went to join the call. Mr. Haywood was laughing heartily at something Mr. Maldonado was saying. "I know, George. I know."

Catherine Haywood looked at her husband and raised both of her hands in the air. She walked away frustrated.

"What?" Brandi asked her. "He was laughing, huh? I guess living like animals is funny to him. I don't find any of this funny."

"Brandi, don't let your father hear you talking that way. Now hush."

Raven looked from her mother to her sister. She hated when they spoke of her father like that. When the thunder roared, the lights went out.

"Great," Mrs. Haywood grumbled. The girls could hear their mother's voice, but they couldn't see her. "I'll get the candles."

Brandi made her way to where Raven was sitting. Her father stood in the doorway with a flashlight. Just as her mother arrived with the candles, it sounded like the roof had opened up. Her father ran to the living room to survey the damage. "We have to go. Girls, go upstairs to pack a bag. This is bad."

When her father's usually playful mood turned serious, they knew they better hurry. "Is it funny now, James?" Mrs. Haywood snapped. That's all the girls heard as they quickly ran upstairs to gather clothing for school. It was difficult to navigate through the house with only a flashlight to guide their way.

"Stay with me, RaRa," Brandi instructed her sister.

"Don't worry, B. I'm too scared to be alone."

Brandi quickly gathered her belongings, and then they went to Raven's room and did the same. "Be careful going down these stairs with your suitcase."

"I am, Bran. I'm not a little girl anymore, you know?"

"Let's talk about it when we get to a warm, dry place. It's not the time to be independent."

"But, Brandi, all I'm saying is ..." They were both hushed as they walked in on their parents trying to use trash bags to cover their furniture.

"Mom!" Brandi yelled. "Daddy!" No matter what they did, there was no recovering any of the items in the living room. Brandi began to gather their pictures off the mantle. She grabbed one of the trash bags and began dumping the pictures into it as Raven stood stunned.

"Let's go, please. Let's just go," Raven cried.

Anything that could be saved had been saved. The rest of the items were worthless within minutes. Furniture that had taken two years to pay off ruined in a matter of seconds. The angels that Mrs. Haywood loved destroyed in the blink of an eye.

They drove away from their home unsure of the condition they would find it in when they returned. It seemed as if the only room damaged was the living room, but there would be a more careful inspection come morning.

They drove slowly through the neighborhood. There was debris everywhere, and the streetlights were still out. It was difficult to navigate, but Mr. Haywood did it—out of the neighborhood and onto the freeway. It looked as though a tornado had visited Port City. They saw enough of them to know its path of destruction.

The family arrived at the Highland Hotel a bit rattled, so they were relieved to see the hotel open for business. Even though it was seriously damaged during the recent hurricane, the owners had made immediate repairs.

The Haywoods were soaked and exhausted when they entered the lobby. The attendants rushed to help them.

"We need a room," Brandi's mother said through tears. Raven looked at her mother, astonished. Catherine Haywood was the person who never cried, and here she was asking for a room with tears dripping from her eyes.

Her father hugged her mother around the shoulder and took their keycard from the receptionist. After taking the elevator to the fourth floor, they walked silently down the hall and put the keycard in the door. It didn't work. They tried again. It still didn't work.

"I'll go down and get a new key," Brandi mumbled and walked away with Raven trailing closely behind.

"Bran?"

"Don't, RaRa. Not right now," Brandi said as the elevator doors closed to shut out Raven. Brandi was ready to explode.

She approached the lobby desk and slapped the keycard down on the counter, even though the receptionist was helping another guest. "It doesn't work."

"Oh, I'm so sorry. Sometimes the weather—"

"Look, I need someone to come up to our room and get the door opened now." She knew that she was being a douche, but she couldn't quell the emotions. The clerk looked only a few years older than

Brandi, and she was only moments away from reacting.

Just as the scene was about to get ugly, a manager stepped in. "I'll show you to your room. Okay, Miss?"

"No. Just Brandi." They walked to the elevator in silence. On the way to the fourth floor, Brandi's attitude changed. "Thanks for helping me. We've been through a lot."

"I understand. If you need anything, please ask for me. I'm on duty all night."

By the time they made it upstairs to her parents, her mother had calmed down. The manager quickly swiped their new keycard and let them into their room.

"Are you okay, Mama?" Raven asked her.

"Mama's fine. Now go get into some dry clothes."

Raven went into the bathroom. Brandi was left with her parents. "I'm leaving," she announced out of the clear blue. She was nodding her head. "I'm leaving Port City for college. Forgive me, but I can't do this anymore."

"Forgive you? I'm happy for you," her father said.

Her mother agreed. "It's time for you to see something different." She brought her voice to a whisper. "You can't live your whole life for your sister. She'll be fine."

Brandi thought about it, and her mother was right. She was trying to live for Raven, but she knew if she didn't leave now, Port City would suffocate her. That wouldn't be good for any of them. Now she had to break the news to a few other people. She wasn't sure if it would go over as well as it did tonight.

# CHAPTER 7

# Shane

Submitting her documentary to every contest in America had been Shane's goal ever since saving her final draft. She knew from her father that selling was a number's game. He had taught her well during his election, and she was determined to find someone who saw the potential in her documentary, called *The Blues*.

She knew that she had a great story, but nothing prepared her for the letter from *Teen Bites*. It was sitting on her bed when she returned home from school. She opened the envelope, expecting rejection.

"Better luck next time," other letters usually read.

She ripped open the envelope, hoping for a word of encouragement, advice, or anything other than a flat-out no. Today was different, though. Today the letter read, "Congratulations! Your documentary has been chosen as one of ten films to compete at *Teen Bites*." She couldn't read any further. She ran down the stairs, screaming her good news.

"Shane, slow down. Good news? Bad news? What?" Her mother asked, half-laughing at her daughter.

"We did it, Mom! We did it!" she exclaimed, shoving the letter into her mother's hand.

"What is wrong with her?" Robin asked, joining them in the kitchen.

"Oh my goodness, Shane, this is awesome," her mother said, passing the letter to Robin.

Robin surveyed the letter. "New York!

I've never even been to New York. Do they need chaperones?"

"I don't know. I'm going to call Mrs. Monroe."

"I'm sure she knows, Shane. Wasn't she in charge of the whole thing?"

"I was the one who submitted to the contests, Mom."

"Oh, baby, I'm so proud of you. You did this on your own?" she asked, surprised. "I'm impressed. I wish I was more like you when I was growing up. Maybe I would be a housewife *and* an entrepreneur today."

"Being the wife of a city councilman is a full time job, Mom," Robin said, jumping to her defense. "Plus, who else could take care of a man, two kids, a grandchild, and secretly write her own cookbook?"

"Robin?" Their mother thought nobody knew about her writing. They were just eating what she cooked. How could they know she was testing recipes? "How did you know?"

"I have my ways. Plus, we are the ones who are being stuffed with all these great desserts. Hello."

"See, I get it from you." Shane kissed her mother and ran up the stairs two at a time to call Mrs. Monroe and give her the good news. When Mrs. Monroe answered the phone, Shane started talking and didn't stop until the whole story was out and the letter was read.

"Well, that was a mouthful," Mrs. Monroe said, laughing. "We have a lot of work to do, Shane. This is only the beginning, but I'm with you." She continued, "You took us this far, and I'll get us to New York. Don't worry about a thing. Get the team ready. Fundraising starts immediately."

"Will do, Mrs. Monroe."

"Hey, Shane, congratulations. Great job."

She couldn't help but be proud of herself. She smiled as Mrs. Monroe complimented her on all of her hard work.

Her mentor and her teacher, she sounded proud.

Shane immediately opened a video chat with her best friends. She was bursting at the seams. "I have news! *The Blues* placed at *Teen Bites* in New York!"

"Ahh!" they all screamed at the same time.

"I wish I could let you go to New York without me," Brandi told her.

"When is it?" Marisa asked.

"Spring break!" Shane exclaimed.

"Spring break?" Marisa said excitedly.

"We are so there," Brandi proclaimed.

"How are you two coming to New York? It's just for the journalism team. We have so much money to raise in such a short period of time. I can't put any more on Mrs. Monroe."

"It won't be on Mrs. Monroe. We will figure it out, but we're coming."

"Oh, I know!" Marisa exclaimed. "Idea. Let's make it the senior trip. They were taking us to D.C. anyway. Let's talk to the powers that be. The whole senior class could go to New York instead."

"I like that!" Shane said, nodding her head. "Okay, we have win over Mrs. Woods and Mrs. Scapin."

"You know that's who Mrs. Monroe kicks it with. That's perfect!" Brandi said, stoked.

"This is going to work. I can just feel it," Marisa said.

"New York City, here we come!" Shane said, believing in their plan.

The next day when they arrived at school, they hurried to the teachers' lounge where they knew Mrs. Monroe would be having coffee with Mrs. Woods and Mrs. Scapin. They softly knocked on the door. The teachers' lounge was considered sacred. No student dared to enter or else they would face suspension. It made them nervous to even knock.

"Girl, you gotta knock harder than that," Brandi said, pushing her to the side.

"Are you sure we should be doing this? Maybe we should wait until—"

The door to the lounge flew open and Coach Davis stood on the other side. "What are you girls doing here?"

"Um ... well," they could hear Mrs. Monroe laughing in the background. "I need to speak to Mrs. Monroe. It's kind of important," Shane said, almost whispering. She felt like they had just crashed a private party and wondered if it was a good idea.

"Is that Shane? What's wrong? What's the matter?" Mrs. Monroe seemed so concerned. This must be important if Shane brought Brandi and Marisa.

"I needed to talk to you about the New York trip, but I wanted to talk to you along with Mrs. Woods and Mrs. Scapin. This was the only way we knew to get all of you together. The day gets so hectic sometimes, and I—"

"One second, Shane." She retreated back into the teachers' lounge.

"I told you this was a bad idea, but nooo ..." Marisa scolded.

"Okay, girls. It's funny you even came here. I was just telling them about *The Blues*. Come in. Come in."

They slowly walked into the lounge— a place that in all their four years at PCH they had never seen. Whatever visions they had of the location, this wasn't it. It was a small room with vending machines, tables, and two microwaves. The laughter that flowed out of the lounge would have you thinking there was a chocolate fountain and ice sculptures, but there were none of those luxuries. They slowly drank in their surroundings, feeling privileged to even be in there.

"That's what we wanted to talk to you about. We have an idea."

"I have an idea, but who needs credit," Marisa said, almost cutting her off.

"Okay, Marisa had an idea," Shane confessed.

"Spit it out, Shane," Brandi told her.

"Do you think we could change the senior trip to New York instead of Washington, D.C.? It would be great if everyone could participate. It's not just my story. It's Port City's story."

"The rooms have already been booked and the itinerary set," Mrs. Woods whispered to Mrs. Scapin. "I'm not sure what the cancelation date is with no penalty."

"We know that everything has already been set in motion, but—" Marisa started.

"But we want to support Shane," Brandi finished. "And there are a lot of other people in our class who would probably feel the same way. Sure, many people wanted to go to our country's capital, but this is New York City." Brandi breathed a big gulp of air. "I don't know many people who have gone to New York. We can go see a play, or watch the taping of a television show. The options in New York are endless. I know I can get other seniors on board."

The teachers whispered for a minute. "Prove it!" a voice said from across the lounge. They were so into the conversation they hadn't even noticed Mr. McAfee, the debate teacher. He had been listening.

"They should bring signatures from the other seniors. If the trip can be changed, this is as worthy a cause as any. You'll have my vote." He nodded approval to Brandi, and she smiled. He had taught her how to make a case, and she had unknowingly convinced him.

"Excellent idea, Mister McAfee. I think that's more than fair," Mrs. Monroe told them, and they all agreed. "You have forty-eight hours to get those signatures. Good luck!"

**CHAPTER 8**

# The Dotted Line

The girls left the teachers' lounge and headed straight to the library. They still had another fifteen minutes before the bell rang for first period. At least they could get their thoughts together and brainstorm their next move.

"Okay, so what do we need to do first?" Marisa questioned her friends.

"I think that we should make a flyer

73

explaining what *Teen Bites* is," Shane told them.

"If we had more time, yes, but they gave us forty-eight hours. That's not a lot of time. What we should do is get a list of the seniors, divide it up, and get the signatures."

"That's a lot of signatures," Marisa said. "We are close to four hundred seniors now."

"Well, I can get the journalism team to help us out," Shane said.

Just then, they heard a loud roar of thunder outside. "Is it supposed to rain today?" Brandi asked nervously, running to the library window. The clouds were gray, and the weather began to change rapidly. A bolt of lightning illuminated the gray skies. "I can't even focus on this," Brandi said, joining her friends back at the table.

"We are almost done. Can you hang in for another second?" Shane asked her.

"Could you? If your family's home took a beating every time it rained?"

"It's going to be okay," Marisa said, trying to console her friend.

"You would say that," Brandi spat. "Your home is just fine ... living high on the hog from your dad's ill-gotten gains."

"Girl, calm down. You going off all Shakespearean-like over there. It's not Mari's fault."

"But she hasn't done anything to make it right." Brandi turned to Marisa. "You act like nothing's even going on. Like my family didn't have to move into a hotel. Like your father hasn't taken my father's money. I've been trying to stay out of this, so I haven't mentioned it. But dang, Mari."

"I wasn't aware that my father's company—"

"You weren't aware that my family's problem is your family's windfall. Don't worry about it. Go out and celebrate. It's on us." Brandi left the library abruptly, separating herself from her friends.

"Well, that didn't go well," Shane said matter-of-factly.

Marisa was silent. A tear rolled down her cheek. "She always blames me. Forget the fact that your father is the one who introduced Papa to that Betancourt character. Forget the fact that your father is just as much to blame for all of this. I'm tired of being a target."

"Marisa!" Shane was surprised. She had never looked at it that way. When Brandi told them about the storm destroying their home, she never put the pieces together. She didn't even realize that the dinner with Mr. Betancourt had been the catalyst. "I never—"

"And nobody ever makes you, Shane," Marisa said, gathering her belongings and walking out of the library in a huff.

Shane sat alone. "What just happened?" she said aloud and went back to work organizing their next steps. One little fight was not about to deter her plans. "Guess I'm on my own. But what's new?"

The bell rang, signaling the beginning of the school day. She gathered her things and walked to her locker alone. Her two friends weren't at their lockers, but she didn't figure they would be. *Let them marinate on it for a sec*, she thought as she headed to class.

When she walked in, the journalism team stood up and began clapping. She was awestruck. Then she realized what was happening. Her cheeks became flushed, giving her away. With a half-smile on her lips, she said, "Thanks, everyone. We did it."

"Don't be modest," Hannah told her, coming to her side. "We helped shoot the video. *You* got us into *Teen Bites*."

Hannah had been on the volleyball team with Shane when Shane had fallen for Coach Rob. During that time, they weren't as close as they were now. But they had bonded this year over the school newspaper. Hannah was managing editor, the same title Shane held the year before. She had taken the role and ran with it. She was a great second-in-command.

Shane wished she had gotten to know Hannah better when they played volley-ball, instead of putting all her energy into her relationship with Coach Rob. But she knew that she couldn't go back. She had closed that chapter.

"Speech. Speech. Speech!" the class began to cheer.

She looked at Mrs. Monroe for approval. Mrs. Monroe smiled brightly at Shane and nodded.

"Thank you all so much. I'm not just saying that I couldn't have done it without you. I *really* couldn't have done it without you. And, my dear seniors, we did it way big!" They all started cheering. "And our journey isn't over. We are going to New York Cit-ay! Now, I have to tell you, some of the other seniors—"

"Brandi and Mari!" someone yelled.

"Yes, Brandi and Mari. We thought it would be a good idea for us to go together: the whole senior class."

There was a hush, and then a unanimous cheer.

"But I need your help. We have to get signatures from the senior class agreeing that it would be in our best interest to move the senior trip from D.C. to New York *and* to move it to spring break."

"That's a lot, Shane," Hannah said. "I mean, what about those people who already have plans for spring break? What happens to them?"

"That's why we are voting. Everybody wasn't going to D.C., and I'm sure everyone won't be going to New York either."

"How much will it cost?"

"We are going to have to do some fund-raising. That's why I'm asking you first. If y'all aren't on board, then it's a no-go."

"Well, I'm down," Dustin Chaisson said from the back of the room. He was another person who Shane had grown fond of. He had her back, even though he had come on a little stronger than she would have liked when they first met.

Dustin was the one who outted Coach Rob and his past misdeeds. After it was all said and done, their friendship fizzled. It just wasn't comfortable anymore, so they didn't force it. Since then, they had love for each other but only from afar. Shane had to admit, it was nice for him to have her back. She smiled his way, and he gave her one simple nod of approval.

After that, everyone else followed suit, giving their agreement. Then they got down to the business of tackling the giant project they had before them. They divided up jobs, played to each other's strengths, and got a solid plan in place. This meeting went much differently than the one with Brandi and Marisa.

It was still stormy outside. They could hear the windows rattling. When it was time to leave class, the bells did not sound. Staff came around with a bullhorn, telling everyone to move to second period. They informed the teachers that the bells were out due to the severe weather.

By the time lunch started, the rain had begun to subside. When the girls sat at their table in the lunchroom, it was obvious that the tension that started between them was not dissipating like the weather. They ate their food in silence.

"How long is this going to go on?" Shane asked out of nowhere, addressing the elephant in the room.

"Ask her," Brandi said, pointing at Marisa.

"Ask me? You act like I fix houses. I'm sorry about your home, but I can't fix it.

Honestly, I don't know if Papa can either." She hung her head in shame.

"It's our money. Your father took our money and bought supplies for his business."

"He gave it to Mister Betancourt, who Mister Foster swore to him was legit. Talk to him about finding that guy."

"Look, my father thought he was helping," Shane joined in.

"Not my family. Couldn't be my family because we live at the Highland Hotel right now. So who was he helping?"

"Okay, it's a mess. I get it." Shane reached across the table and grabbed both their hands. "We are going to figure this out, but we have to do it together. Come on," she pleaded with her friends. "We won't get anything done if we are beefin' with each other. This is about our fathers, not us."

"Okay, but we have to figure it out. My home means everything to me," Brandi told them.

## CHAPTER 9

# *Brandi*

*B*randi stood on the stage of Central High School with the rest of the people on the debate team. This was the year that she was supposed to lead her team all the way to state. She thought when she arrived at this moment, it would be so simple. She knew she had the talent to win, but her life was in turmoil right now.

Just yesterday, city workers had put a blue tarp on their roof. Their home looked like many in Port City. Their home was unlivable. They had a lot of work to do before they could move back. Luckily, their insurance company paid for the hotel. However, it was getting cramped in that little room. The only thing they wanted was to go back home, but it was too dangerous. There was too much damage to the roof.

With that weighing on her, Brandi didn't feel like herself. As she stood at the podium, she knew she wasn't giving the team her best. She was not on her A-game, which threw them off. They were losing this competition, and it was obvious.

She sensed that Mr. McAfee was somewhere close in the audience, but she dared not look for him. She could feel his disappointment. She was embarrassed. The longer the competition went on, the more she wanted to run from the building.

When they gave their closing remarks, they knew they had lost. The judges took only minutes to give the win to Central High School. They left the auditorium to get onto the bus in silence. As they stood in line to board, Mr. McAfee stopped Brandi.

"What happened up there?"

"I ... I don't know."

"Well, figure it out. If you aren't up to lead this group, then I'll give your position to someone else."

She studied her shoes. "I understand." She wanted to cry. She didn't want to get on the bus with her team, but she had to. She sat in a seat by herself and stared out the window. They passed some of the most beautiful scenery in Texas. It was cold, and frost was on the grass. They pulled up to Mazzio's Pizzeria to eat dinner before heading back to school. Brandi asked Mr. McAfee if she could stay on the bus for some alone time. He said yes.

When she was alone, she began to sob. She called her mother.

"Mommy ..."

"Baby, what's wrong?"

"Can you come and pick me up?"

"Where are you?"

"I'm on the bus … at Mazzio's. Please, can you come?"

"I'm on my way."

It took Catherine Haywood ten minutes to get there. Her mom went inside the restaurant to let Mr. McAfee know she would be taking Brandi home. She spoke with him briefly, detailing what Brandi had been going through. He understood.

"What happened today, baby?"

"Mama, it's just so much. It's like … I don't know. Like my life is in pieces right now, and I can't make it all come together again."

"I couldn't have said it better myself. I feel the same way, but don't worry. Dad and I have it all under control. I promise. Now, you focus on you, and we will be out of the hotel in no time," she said, pulling up to the Highland Hotel.

"Mom, can I get a minute? I need to make a call."

"Of course, but hurry. It's cold out here. I don't want you to freeze."

"It's not that cold, Mom." As soon as she was alone, she called Erick. "Hey, it's me. You have a minute?"

"For you? Of course."

"I messed up today. We had the debate against Central, and I let my problems overwhelm me. I feel like I let the team down."

"Central? Bran, you handled their seniors last year. It was just a bad day. Don't beat yourself up about it."

"Yeah."

"Plus, you'll have a chance to redeem yourself at the state competition, and you are going to be great."

She smiled, wishing that she could have used the video chat to talk to him.

"You are magnificent, beautiful, and I love every fiber of your soul."

"Erick ..."

"Hey, you don't have to say it back. I

know it's the first time I've said it, but I thought you should know. I love you, Bran. I always will."

"How did I find you?" Brandi was mystified. He was such an awesome guy.

"I kinda found you, feeling a little like you feel right now. Remember that?"

"Yeah, I remember," she said, smiling as she pictured the two of them last year. She had been through a lot and was guarding her feelings. When he asked her to go to Jerry's, she had pounced on him.

"It will get better, Bran. You're just in a rough spot. I wish I could make it better."

"You just did, Erick. I wish I could be there with you."

"No you don't. If you did, you would be."

"You're right." At that moment a light-bulb went off. "I want to be with you too. So that's where I'm going to be."

"Are you saying what I think you're saying? Are you coming to UT in the fall?"

She could hear the smile in his voice. "That's what I'm saying, Erick. Hey, I've gotta go. It's really cold in this car."

"You're just going to drop that on me and get off the phone? Wait! Did you just say that you are in a car? Woman, get in the hotel."

"Okay, okay, and Erick? I love you too." She hung up the phone feeling renewed, happy even. It had been a long time since her smile reached her heart, and Erick was the reason. She wished that she could be at UT right now.

**CHAPTER 10**

# Marisa

Marisa was exhausted after her photo shoot. She was happy to be working. The shoot was for Honda, and it had been a welcome break from Port City. There was a time when the other PCH students had celebrated her success, now they thought she was haughty. But she was far from haughty. It was an assumption that affected her. She wished that they knew her and not the girl in the magazines.

"Mom, I can't go back to school today. I'm too tired," Marisa complained.

"Mari, I'm tired too," her mom said.

"These drives are exhausting. At least let's go by the school and pick up your assignments."

Marisa sighed. She needed a break from Shane and Brandi. Another altercation could be around the corner, and she wasn't in the mood. She didn't want to admit to her mom that the reason she didn't want to go to school was because she didn't want to see her best friends.

Brandi was upset with her about her home, something Marisa had no control over. On the other hand, Shane sat back and allowed her to take the blame, knowing that her father was just as responsible for the lack of construction materials.

"Okay, I'll go to school, but please let's stop and get some lunch before I go." She was happy to buy herself some time. She ate at Paco's Tacos before heading back to the school. They had the best street tacos, and they were only a dollar. Who could beat that?

She signed in at the office before going to her fourth period class. She walked into her English IV class, handed the teacher her pass, and took her seat. It felt good having a place to go to just be still and think. Although she hadn't wanted to come to school, she was happy that she had.

When she sat down, there was a note on her desk. She didn't think it was for her because she was just getting to class. But she opened it anyway to see where it should go. It read, "Give your daddy some of that modeling money so he can stop cheating my family out of ours. Your father's a thief and so are you. You should have died with Bethany."

Her eyes practically popped out of her head. What cruel words. They cut her in so many ways. She looked around the room. Who wrote this vicious note? Nobody was looking at her. They were deeply engrossed in their assignments—or pretending to be. She had to get out of this classroom.

"Mrs. Mitchell, I'm not feeling so well. May I have a pass to the nurse?" she asked, giving the best sick-and-in-pain look that she could muster.

Mrs. Mitchell wrote her a pass without a second thought. Marisa looked back at her classmates, but none of them looked up. *You can all bite me!* she thought as she left.

She didn't want to talk to Shane, and she definitely couldn't talk to Brandi. She went to find the next best person: Romero. She found him in world geography and walked in. She explained to his teacher that she was very ill and needed help from her brother.

"What's wrong with you?" he asked, concerned about his sister.

She led him to the auditorium without speaking. When she got there, she burst into tears. He held his sister as she cried. She was usually the one to rescue him, not the other way around. This was new to both of them, but he held her as if he were the big brother.

"Mari, talk to me. You need me to beat some fool down?" he asked her.

"I don't even know, Rom." She passed him the note that was waiting for her on her desk.

"Aw, man, that's messed up. They have no idea what we've been through, Mari. Don't let them get in your head. Half of the girls in this school are jealous of you. This is a note from one of them. Girls are just messy and dumb. I can't believe they are blaming Papa for all of this."

"Who else would they blame?"

"Mister Foster for one. You know how all of this went down. Or Mister Betancourt, wherever he is."

"Papa is the easy target. He's the contractor. You know that. Mister Foster has too much pull, and Mister Betancourt can't even be located. Please. The Maldo-nados have already been in enough trouble over these few years. Papa is the fall guy."

"Find out who sent this, and I'll shove it down their stupid throats."

"Well, what are you going to do to Brandi? Because she feels the same way. She's not even talking to me."

"Brandi? Yeah, girls are wack. That's why I just get it in and I'm done."

"Ew. Please don't ever say that to me again. Ever," Marisa said.

Romero laughed at his sister. She was so sweet, innocent, and sometimes naïve. Street smart she wasn't. That's why he wanted to just bust fools in the head when it came to her. She was too sweet to pick on, but people could find fault with anybody.

"Hey, you think you'll be okay to make it through the rest of the day, or do you want me to call Mom? I'll make her understand. It's up to you."

"I'm okay, Rom. Thanks for being here

for me. I never thought I'd see the day when you would have to take care of me." She smiled at him. He was taller than her now and obviously sexually active. The thought made her cringe. She could see her baby brother turning into a man. He would be the oldest sibling at home come fall. It was hard to believe. Very hard.

"I'm going back to class. I have a meeting today anyway," she said.

"Okay, I'll walk you to class."

By the time they left, the bell was ringing for fifth period. They were both getting weird looks as they walked down the hallway. "Maldonados are thieves!" one kid screamed out. "Liars!"

"Go back to Mexico, thieves!"

That one did it. Romero turned around and decked some kid. He fell to the ground as if he had never been hit in his life.

"Rom! No!" Marisa yelled. She hadn't been trying to get her brother in trouble. "Oh my God! Stop!"

"Keep the name Maldonado out yo mouth, *vato!*" he yelled as the boy looked up at him, regretting joining in with the others.

The assistant principal showed up and hustled Romero to the office. Marisa sent her mother a text letting her know what was going on. But it was their father who showed up at the principal's office. Marisa met him there.

"Go back to class, mi hija. You should be getting your education, not in here with me."

"No, Papa. This is my fault." She showed him the note and explained what had happened.

"Well, it looks like I'm the one to blame. Let me talk to the principal a bit."

They walked in the office and the secretary greeted Mr. Maldonado coldly. Her home was not complete either. She was another disgruntled customer. *Great*, Marisa thought, watching her dad handle the situation.

"Daddy, please let me go in too? Please?" she begged him. He finally relented.

They sat down across from Mrs. Montgomery, realizing that she was no longer on their side. It was a cold day for the Maldonado family. Marisa tried to explain away her brother's reaction. She even showed her the letter, but Mrs. Montgomery had already made up her mind. Romero would be attending the Port City Alternative Center.

"This is his first offense, Mrs. Montgomery. Surely—"

"Surely there's a lesson that he needs to learn. This is a nonviolent facility, Mister Maldonado, and there are no exceptions."

"I will go to the school board."

"Go ahead. You'd be hard-pressed to find a sympathetic ear in this town, especially with so many people under duress. They're more concerned about their own families right now."

Her words sank in and hit hard. People were now taking this out on his children. He slowly stood to his feet. "I'll be taking my children home today, Mrs. Montgomery. Thanks for your time."

When they got to the car, he immediately called Mr. Foster. "Brian, we need to talk. I'm taking my children home, then I'll be right there." Marisa could tell that her father was angry. He clutched the steering wheel as his knuckles turned white. "Papa's going to make this right," her father said. "Don't worry about anything. I'll make it right."

Marisa knew that he would. It was his job. He always took care of them, and the last thing he would do was let somebody come along and ruin everything he'd worked so hard for. Mr. Betancourt had no idea, but he had messed with the wrong guy.

# CHAPTER 11

# *Shane*

The seniors were overjoyed when they found out they would be going to New York. Shane and the rest of the journalism team had obtained all necessary signatures in twenty-four hours instead of the forty-eight hours promised them.

The next step had been setting up the first fundraiser, which was right up Shane's alley. She had helped during her father's campaign and knew what it took to have successful fundraisers. The first one she planned was at the Room. She knew she would need to do something fun.

She talked to the owner and got the venue donated. She had a list of DJs in the area and couldn't decide which one would be most likely to work pro bono, so she started making calls. So many of them already had parties on the planned day, and she was getting frustrated. She thought she would never find a DJ.

She got to the bottom of her list. *Last name ... this has to work.*

"This is Nigel," she heard the masculine voice say.

"Hi, Nigel. We are doing a fundraiser for the PCH senior trip the last weekend of this month and need a DJ. Are you available that weekend?"

"Let me look at my calendar."

"I have to tell you, this is a pro bono gig. It's for a good cause, though," she began to talk quickly. "It's our senior trip. My documentary ... well, our documentary, won a place at *Teen Bites*."

"Wow, that's impressive. What's the name of your documentary?"

"*The Blues*. It documents everything that we went through during Hurricane Adam, and how we came to the point of having seventy percent of our citizens with blue rooftops."

"What's your name again?"

"Shane. Shane Foster."

"Shane? This is DJ Dazed. Do you remember me? We met at—"

"The Room! How could I forget?"

"Good memory."

"When it's important," she responded.

"Well, maybe we should catch a bite to eat, and you can let me know exactly what you need."

"Is that a yes? You'll do it?" she asked.

"You'll have dinner with me?"

"I'm mad that it took you this long to ask me, so yeah," she said, smiling as she smoothed her hair in her bathroom mirror.

"Well then, count me in, and I'll see you tonight," he said.

"Tonight?"

"Like you said, this was a long time coming, so let's get on with this before Port City is only a memory for you, because I have a feeling that you'll never live here again after this year."

She chuckled. "You might be right about that. Tonight it is."

From that moment on, they were together. That dinner turned into two weeks of dating—two inseparable weeks leading up to the first fundraiser. The night of the party, Shane stayed by his side. She was on the microphone more than him. Everyone showed up. They played *The Blues* on the big screen in the back of the club. The mood was celebratory.

As midnight approached, the lights were turned up. Everyone began making after-party plans. Nigel asked Shane,

Marisa, and Brandi to join him at Waffle House. When they got there, it was packed with people.

They saw Matthew Kincade and his group eating breakfast with a group of freshman girls who looked to be just their type. Cute, young, and high school hopeful. They still had that high-school-is-the-best-place-ever look. It was reminiscent of how Shane, Brandi, and Marisa used to be. They had long ago lost their new car smell.

They smiled, knowing that it used to be them sitting in those very booths with upperclassmen. They could see the basketball team: Trent, Ashton, and all their friends staying out until two o'clock in the morning. Yeah, they had their fun. Now they just wanted a good meal, a good man, and some rest. They never thought they would see the day when they were too tired to kick it, but that day had arrived.

After they were done with their food, Brandi and Marisa rode home together, and Shane left with Nigel. They headed to the seawall to watch the boats come in and get some alone time. "Your friends are going to be mad that you left them."

"We are too old for that. Plus, they need a little time alone. They are going through a rough patch, the two of them."

"Not you?"

"Nah, I mean ... not really."

"So, what's your next step, Miss Foster? After you win your contest and everything."

"I really don't know. I've applied to several colleges, but I haven't heard back from any of them yet. If all else fails, I'll be at Baymont."

"Baymont? I don't see you staying out here."

"Why are you still in Port City, Nigel?"

"I don't know. My business ... my name. I'm heading to Houston as soon as I get my name more recognized out there. I'm working on it."

"Houston's cool, but—" He silenced her with a kiss.

"I saw a shooting star, sorry," he said when they finally pulled away.

"Aren't you supposed to make a wish?" she asked, smiling.

"That was my wish, Shane Foster."

She laughed. "How did we miss all of this time together? You could have stopped me from making some stupid mistakes."

"Like what?"

"Like, I'd rather be kissing you than talking about the past. I'm here with you now, in the present. Now let's make the best of it." She leaned over and kissed him again, just as a barge entered the port, sending waves splashing against the rocks. It was romantic. They had flirted with this opportunity for years, and here they were, together.

## CHAPTER 12

# Can I Get a Break?

Shane, Brandi, and Marisa met with Mrs. Monroe to discuss how they should utilize the monies that had already been allotted for their trip. At this point, they were just making up the difference. The senior class had already paid for their portion. They were just filling in the gaps with the money they raised. New York was a tad more expensive than D.C., and they had to make adjustments. The last thing they wanted was a New York trip on a shoe-string budget.

"So, ladies, we have to take the money from the other fundraiser and put it to the side for the link sale. Let's allot five hundred dollars. We won't use all of it, but at least it will be there." Mrs. Monroe was good about walking them step-by-step through the process.

They had always wanted to make a mark on the school. *The Blues* had them well on their way there. Which senior class would follow them and top that?

"Got it," Shane said, jotting down the last of the notes from their meeting.

"Jerry's! Jerry's!" Brandi cheered.

"Dudette, I gotta get home," Shane told them. "Plus, it's lasagna night, and I'm 'bout that lasagna life."

"Ooh, girl, me too! To the Foster house. Let's jet."

"That's a bet! Moms is cooking two pans anyway," Shane said.

"Fat, fat, and more fat. Y'all want me to never model again?" Marisa whined.

"She's making salad too."

"Okay. I'll just have a small bite of lasagna. A salad with a side of lasagna, please."

"Only you," Brandi told her.

They pulled up at the Foster house, but a car that Shane had never seen before sat in the driveway. "Looks like we have company," Shane said, putting her little beat-up car in park. *I hope Mom's not upset that I'm bringing my friends home without telling her,* Shane thought.

Their company was on his way out when they were walking in. Shane could hear her father's voice. "Now *I'm* being investigated? I had nothing to do with the money. I never saw a penny of it."

"Here's my card, Mister Foster. Call me if you remember anything that can help in our investigation."

They looked at each other as the FBI

agent exited the Foster home. "Mom, is it a good time—"

"When is it not a good time for Brandi and Marisa? Everything is fine. Right, Brian?"

"Yeah. Fine. I'll be in my office. Put my plate to the side." There wasn't just an elephant in the room. There were hundreds.

"Excuse me. I have to call my mom," Marisa said, hurriedly leaving the room. When she returned, she was in tears. "Papa is being investigated. An FBI agent just left my house too. What are we going to do? Our fathers are going to take the fall for this man."

"Marisa," Mrs. Foster said, coming by her side. "You don't worry about any of this. One thing we all have on our side is right. Brian and George did nothing wrong. They just trusted the wrong person. In the end, they will be vindicated."

She was so calm that she calmed

them down too. It was as if her voice, her words, had some sort of tranquilizer effect on them. There was a peace in the room that wasn't there before. "Now, I'll fix your plates. Salad only, Mari?"

"No, ma'am. I need carbs after all of this. Bring on the lasagna," she said, laughing.

They ate until their bellies hurt. Robin, Gavin, and Aiden walked in soon after they had finished.

Gavin balanced their bags from the mall on one side and a two-year-old Aiden on the other while Robin chatted feverishly on the phone.

"Auntie! Auntie!" Aiden yelled when he saw Shane, reaching out for her.

"Get off the phone, Robie," Shane told her.

"Shane, hush. Anyway, girl, that was just Shane."

Shane crossed the kitchen now holding Aiden. "No, for real. Get off the phone before Mommy comes back in here."

"Hey, I gotta go," Robin said seriously. "What? Why you trippin'?" she asked Shane.

"The Feds were here today. Is that reason enough to trip?"

"For what?" Robin asked, shocked.

"For Daddy. Remember that Betancourt guy who had dinner over here? He made that deal for all those building supplies, right? He was a con artist or something, and he took the FEMA money. They can't find him."

"What? And they believe Daddy's involved?"

"And my father," Marisa added, nodding her head.

Robin sat down on the stool as Gavin fixed their dinner plates. "This is unbelievable," she cried.

"Mom swears everything is under control. She's in there with Daddy now."

"This is a classic case of out of control," Robin said, disagreeing with her mother. "Look, one thing is for sure. You all don't need to worry about it. I mean, what will that change?" She took the first bite of her food. "Dang, Mom cuts up on some lasagna."

"Right?" Brandi said, looking up from her phone.

"Hey, I hope you are not over there on Friender. We not gonna look for you this time if yo trifling behind goes missing," Robin teased.

"Robin, you get on my last nerve." Brandi threw a piece of bread her way.

"Nah, I'm just kidding. We would look for you. Again. Get off da phone, k?" she mumbled under her breath. "Ain't nobody got time for all that."

With Robin, there was never a dull moment. She was like the smartest, coolest girl any of them had ever met. She had gotten pregnant with Aiden her senior year, but she was still determined to make something out of herself.

When she got a job at Dillard's as a

buyer, it was a no-brainer. Her family had always pegged her as a budding engineer, but the girl could shop. She was living her dream. She always came in with bags of clothing she acquired at cost. They gave her an insane discount, and she came home with the most unique, cutting-edge ensembles. She was still the three girls' idol, even though they were seniors now.

"So, the link sale. What else needs to be done? I gotta get home," Brandi told them.

"Now that yo belly full, you gotta get home? Ole hungry behind," Robin said, still in the mood to pick on Brandi.

"You gonna ease up on me tonight. Don't be mad cuz my daddy is not being investigated. We are the ones living under a blue roof because of all y'all's drama."

"Touché!" Robin said, laughing. "You got me on that one, but at least we can laugh about it."

"Man, y'all crazy. This some serious

stuff," Gavin told them. "I've never even met a federal agent, and I don't want to either."

"Me neither," Marisa said. "I really should get home too. I want to check on Papa. I know, I know ... don't worry about it. I'll just feel better when I hear it from him."

"Come on. Let's get you girls to the crizib," Shane said, grabbing her keys. "You think Daddy could buy me a new car with all his stolen money?"

"Shane, not really funny," Robin said.

"Y'all make a joke, it's funny. I make a joke? I go too far."

"It was a little too far," Brandi joined in with Robin.

"I'm done. Now y'all on the same side?" Shane laughed. "Let's roll."

## CHAPTER 13

# Marisa

When Marisa stepped her foot outside of Shane's car, she wanted to run to her front door. She entered quickly and surveyed the scene. Her sisters were watching television in the living room. Her brother was tucked away in his own room, and her parents sat closely in the kitchen with e-mails and paperwork from their company, Mi Casa es Su Casa.

"What happened?"

"Marisa, this doesn't concern you. We are helping them with their investigation.

That's it. They are going to find this man. People don't just vanish."

"They do if they are from Haiti, and that's where he's from. He's like a voodoo ghost. There's no telling where he is at this point," Marisa complained.

Marisa's father spoke sternly to her. "Leave this alone, Marisa. You sound too involved to me."

"But, Papa ..."

"No!" her father yelled, hitting the table. "You have had to take on more than your share for this family." He softened as he looked at his daughter. "This is your senior year. Now enjoy it, mi hija. Don't worry about your old man. I have been taking care of myself for many moons."

A tear dropped from her eye as she knelt down beside her father. "But how can I, Papa?"

"Find a way. Don't give it another thought." He smoothed the wayward strands of hair that stuck to her tear-streaked face. "And I believe a letter may have come for you today." Her father smiled. "I put it on your bed."

"From where?" She stood up excitedly.

"Go see."

She ran to her room. The University of Arkansas! She ripped the letter open and read as if it were the last thing she would ever read. A smile crept to her face. "I'm going to Arkansas," she said aloud.

Isi stood in her doorway. "Where's Arkansas again?" she asked.

Marisa was so engrossed in the letter that she didn't know that her youngest sister had joined her. She turned around to face her. "It's not too far."

"Is that where Trent is too? Are you going to be with him?"

"Those are a lot of questions from a little girl. But yes and yes." She walked out of her room and shared her letter with her parents. "I got in!"

"Mi hija," her mother said, grabbing her

face. She had come to this country unable to speak English, but she was determined that her children would have more. No matter what she had to sacrifice, she was willing to do it for her babies.

Her father grabbed her like she was still a little girl. He held her away and looked at her intently. "This isn't for that tall boy, is it? It's for you."

"Yes ... I mean ... I think so." She was so caught up in the moment that she hadn't taken the time to ask herself that question.

The next day she brought the letter with her to school. She wanted to share the news with Shane and Brandi.

"Mari, this is great."

"We are really doing this. We are really going to be spread out all over this country," Brandi said, pouting.

"I'm going to miss my girls," Shane told them. "I need to figure out what's going on with me. Bran is headed to UT. You are gonna be a Razorback. I'm gonna be right here babysitting Aiden. Lawd."

"Yeah, you always get the short end of the stick," Brandi said sarcastically.

Shane wasn't as worried as she pretended to be. She knew that a door would open. She just wished that it would open up a little bit quicker.

While they were celebrating Marisa's good news over lunch, Ashley walked over to their table.

"Hey, Marisa. I see you got a YOU of A letter. I just left from visiting there this weekend. Did Trent tell you?"

"Of course," Marisa lied smoothly.

"It was nice of him to show me around. I'm so excited about going there. It was a beautiful campus."

"So you were accepted?"

"Yes, I found out about a month ago. Maybe we can be roomies."

"And then hell will freeze over," Shane mumbled under her breath.

"Oh, Shane," Ashley mocked her.

"Oh, Ashy," Shane responded back.

"Haven't we mended fences?" Brandi jumped in. "Chill," she said, looking Shane's way.

"Well, that's great news, Ashley. Congratulations," Marisa said politely.

She was furious. She was putting all of her eggs in Trent's basket, and he was still up to his old tricks. The last thing she wanted was to wind up in Arkansas with him and his cheating ways. As soon as Ashley left them, she was ready to open up to her girls.

"He's still at it. I can't go out there like this. I don't trust him, and I definitely don't trust *her*. Now we are all going to be together in Arkansas. I can't do it."

"Where else did you apply?"

"Julliard and University of Houston."

"Have you heard back from them?"

"Not a word."

"You will. Girl, you come from praying

parents. Everything happens for a reason," Shane told her.

"You are starting to sound like your mother," Brandi laughed.

"It's because I'm so mature now," Shane said with an eye roll.

"What are you going to tell Trent?" Brandi asked Marisa.

"Nothing. Just like he told me about his little visit with Ashley."

"So you didn't know?"

"That's my girl!" Shane exclaimed. "Forget that fool. He had a top model and wanted to holler at a hood rat."

"I don't think Ashley would be considered a hood rat," Marisa said.

"Why? She has been through my hood a couple of times that I know of," Brandi told her.

"Mine too," Shane said, dapping her friend up. "And ... you best stop trying to take up for her while she playing sleepless in Arkansas with your dude."

"I don't have claims on him like that," Marisa confessed.

"But you're going to Arkansas to be with him?" Shane asked.

"No, I'm not ... I'm not going to Arkansas to be with him per se."

"Yeah, you are, mami. And if you think you aren't, then you have to really do some soul searching. You are so far from the modeling world in Arkansas."

"Shane's right. You built your career here. You either stay close to H-Town, or you head off to New York. At least that's the plan for you. The Arkansas plan? That's for him."

Her girls were right. Their words sat with her through the rest of the day. She couldn't focus on studying for an upcoming test. All she could think about was Trent. He was in her thoughts yet again.

She decided she needed to have a face-to-face with him. She couldn't just call him. She needed to see his reactions. She decided that FaceTime was necessary and called him. When he picked up the phone and she saw that smile, she could feel it in her toes. She cursed herself. *The boy has me by the soul,* she thought.

"Hey."

"Hey back. How are you out there in Port City?" he asked.

"I'm holding. Look, we have to talk about something, so I'm just going to spit it out. Ashley came to Arkansas to see you?"

"Nah, you know it wasn't like that. She came to see the campus because she got her letter of acceptance and had never even visited."

"Um-hm ... tell me anything, Trent."

"You think I got it like that? That I could get a girl who ain't even my girl to move away from her family and friends to come be with me? She coming to Arkansas to be my number two? Marisa, think about it.

You trippin'. You letting them two nosy ass friends of yours back up in our business. You know I love them, but sometimes I think they want us to break up."

"You real slick! Don't make this about my girls! This is about you and Ashley. Again! How can we be arguing about Ashley? I can see you now, all leaned up against the locker while she dripping on your every word. I remember like it was yesterday."

"You are too pretty to be so damned insecure. And when it comes to Ashley, you are really insecure."

"The last thing walking through the Maldonado house is insecurity. Know that! But you know what I'm gonna do? I'm gonna take this little paper they sent me from Arkansas and rip it up. My insecure ass is going to be somewhere where I don't have to question if I made the right decision. And that's not with you and definitely not in Arkansas."

"Mari! Mari, wait!" she heard him saying.

"I don't have time for that," she said as she disconnected their call. She was going to figure her way out of this and do something amazing. Right now she just didn't know what that was, but she was determined to figure it out.

## CHAPTER 14

# Brandi

With the Haywood house temporarily patched up, Brandi snuggled in her own bed. *This is way better than the hotel,* she thought. Then she heard her phone ring. She groaned. The last thing she wanted was to get up to answer it. *It could be important,* she thought.

Once she gave in to the urge to find out who was calling, she was mad at herself. It was Dub. She had missed his first call, but he wasn't the type to give up easily. She answered the second time. "What, Dub?"

"Is that any way to greet your king?"

"My what?" she snorted. No matter how mad she was at him, he could always find a way to make her laugh and draw her back in. He was the magnet, and she was always fully magnetized. "Boy, one day I'm not going to answer your calls at all."

"Don't play with me, Bran. When I come off tour, you are who I'm coming home to. I don't care if you are wifed up or not. You mine."

"Get a life, Dub. That's never going to happen."

"Yeah, we'll see. Let me see what you rocking over there all cozied up in your bed."

"Stop playing with me, Dub. What you want?"

"Just wanted to take my hot chocolate out for some hot chocolate. Plus, I have a gift for you."

"You do?"

"Yeah, so come outside."

"Why? We just got back in the house. I want to enjoy it."

"Come outside. You know I'm getting my unpredictable on."

She threw on her warm-up pants, grabbed her matching hoodie out of the closet, slipped into her gray Uggs, and ran downstairs. "Going to Starbucks!" she yelled.

"I wanna come, Bran!" she heard Raven yell, but she had to go this one alone.

"Where's my ish?" she asked, jumping into his black Cadillac truck with the peanut-butter-colored interior. The seats were already heated for her. He turned on the massager too. "Boy, stop wining and dining me. I know this ain't gonna last. We have been here before, Dub. Just know I ain't falling for—"

He leaned over and shushed her with a kiss. He pulled away breathlessly. "You talk too much."

"Whatever." In usual Young Dub fashion, he was listening to his own music in the truck. "You don't have anything else to listen to?"

"No, and you don't either. Sit back and let me drive." He turned the music up even louder.

Everyone was looking at them as they rode down the Port City streets. They all knew it was Young Dub driving, but they didn't know who was sitting in the heated seat next to him. Brandi put on her shades and kept her own eyes from wandering. *Let 'em wonder*, she thought as they sped down the strip. She had to admit, after all the drama, she needed a getaway. Yes, she loved Erick, but he was all the way in Austin. She needed an escape, and Dub was it right now.

He pulled into the Starbucks drive-through. "Let me get two hot chocolates, two packs of Madeleines, and one cheese Danish."

"Boy, what's wrong with you? I don't want a hot chocolate." She leaned over him and yelled into the microphone, "Ma'am, cancel one of those hot chocolates and give me a non-fat white chocolate mocha, decaf, light whip, extra hot."

"Dang, cancel my hot chocolate too. I'll have what she's having. B, you as complicated as that drink. You know that?"

"Not really, Dub. You just haven't taken time but to scratch the surface of who I am. You too busy hollering at dirty foots to know when you are with a queen. Don't let the Port City roots fool you. I'm going to be somebody one day."

"I know that already. That's why you the only thing I keep coming back to. Nobody has me like you, Bran, but you scare me."

"I scare you? Boy, hand me my coffee. Young Dub is scared of nothing. At least that's what your songs claim."

As they drove, he said, "Young Dub

may not be scared, but Devin is. You know that already, though."

"You need to be scared of all those pictures of you blazed outta yo mind on Friender. You don't think the cops looking at your Friender page? You are the hottest rapper in Port City, Dub. You have to be more careful."

"You know yo boy just gotta get his mind right sometimes. I just get turnt up for the studio. I flow better that way."

"I never understand why people have to put the evidence on Friender. Just don't get in trouble. I can't represent you yet. When I pass the bar exam, I'll take care of you."

"What will your husband say?"

"He's gonna say: all right."

"He gonna be a weenie anyways. You can't go from a real ninja to a weenie."

"You talk like we are together. We are just friends, Dub."

"Would a friend kiss you like this?"

he asked as he gently kissed her. Horns began to blow as they kissed through the green light, making all the other cars wait behind them.

"Boy, get me home before I forget I'm wearing this purity ring," she cried, laughing. She felt that kiss in her big toe.

Instead of taking her home, he drove deeper into the north side of Port City. He parked his truck in front of a set of gray townhomes that had just been built. She had been here before with her mother, who just had to see what they looked like inside. There was a man-made pond, and all of the townhomes had a view of it from their backyards. "Home is where the heart is, B. I know you've heard that before. Now, let's go get your gift."

She was reluctant. She didn't want to get out of the truck. The last time she had this kind of surprise, she was held captive for nearly two months. If Dub knew her at all, he would have known this was making her feel uncomfortable. "Whose house is this? I am not getting out at some random—"

"Girl, this is home, and these are your keys to the castle. I just bought it, and it needs a woman's touch. Now get on Friender and get some decorating ideas on that li'l girlie app that y'all get on. Get your DIY on, or your decorating on ... whatever."

She thought about the condition of her own home. This would be a wonderful place to come and just kick back. She needed this, wanted this ... shoot, all of the above. *What if Erick finds out?* She wondered if she could make him understand. Not likely.

When she finally ventured out of the truck, she walked into his townhouse. It was spare, with little furniture. Definitely a bachelor's pad. She walked out to the deck. She heard the ducks quacking, frogs croaking, and crickets chirping. It was so peaceful and serene. She took a deep breath in the night air. Dub hugged her, and they looked out over the pond.

"Just breathe, mami. This is all us."

"But, Dub, we aren't even ..."

"Stop worrying about all of that. Live in this moment with me right now."

She kissed him like she never had before. She leaned her head back as he kissed her neck and drank in the moment just as he suggested.

# CHAPTER 15

# Shane

As the weather changed to spring, the realization that there was nothing left to do before the New York trip began to sink in. Shane was free—free to shop, get her hair done, and get packed for a whirlwind week with her senior class.

She was in bed, fuzzy slippers on, enjoying her Saturday. She felt good. What she had accomplished was no small feat. Now that the dust had settled and everything was in place, it was time to enjoy. She slowed down to drink in the day.

The only thing that brought her

uncertainty was the fact that she had no place to call her own for the fall. As other students in her class slowly started getting their acceptance letters, she still hadn't heard back from anywhere. At this point, she had accepted her own fate: college in Baymont. She even toyed with the idea of getting one of those cute little apartments that they had on campus. It wasn't a horrible alternative.

There was a knock on her bedroom door, but she didn't want to answer. She pretended to be asleep. If it wasn't Aiden's little knock, then they couldn't come in, bottom line. Another knock. Then she heard footsteps retreating from the door.

Suddenly, a piece of paper slid under her door. *Now they've resorted to passing notes.* She jumped out of her bed and crept across the room. She didn't want to give away the fact that she had been awake the whole time and was hiding out from her own family.

She tried to focus on what the note read, but it wasn't a note at all. It was a letter from UCLA. *Omigod! Omigod! Omigod!* She ripped it open as quickly as she could. She imagined what it must say. She didn't want to assume. She read. She skimmed. She made it to the most important word of all: congratulations.

Shane began dancing and screaming. She ran downstairs to her mother. "Mommy! Mommy!" Her mother didn't turn around until she was done putting a pie into the oven. "Mom-eeee!" she yelled, shaking her to get her attention.

"Ooh, you're awake now?" her mother asked sarcastically.

"Mommy, I got in to UCLA. UCLA! Do you know what this means?"

"That my baby is leaving me. It means that my baby is moving all the way to California."

"Yes, your baby is lee-ving!" She danced until she was out of breath. She didn't even notice her mother's tears as she set the timer on the oven. "Mommy, you're not happy for me?" she asked, seeing her mother's tears for the first time. "I'm getting away from here. I'm going to see something besides the Port City strip. You *have* to be happy for me."

"I am, baby. You'll understand when you have your own children. The only thing I see right now is you leaving *me*, not Port City."

"No, you can't look at it like that. I never wanted this right now. I wanted to go to PCC, but I can't. Now, I have to make the most of this. It's my destiny."

Mrs. Foster grabbed Shane and hugged her tightly. "My little girl is leaving me. I'm going to be okay." She released her. "You're coming home every holiday." Her mother wiped the tears from her face. "Do you hear me? I don't want to hear you're taking a trip with friends. I'll pay for your ticket— Thanksgiving and Christmas. Promise?"

"I promise! I'm going to call the girls!"

They were just as excited as Shane and just as torn as Mrs. Foster. "This is really it, huh?" Marisa asked.

"This is it. Promise to visit me in L.A.?"

"Every chance I get, and you better not come home for summer. I'm taking courses at UCLA every summer," Brandi told her.

"That's a wonderful idea. We'll just find out which classes will transfer and voilà, together again."

"Count me in. I've never heard a better plan. The industry is on hiatus during the summer, but I'll figure something out," Marisa said excitely.

"What? Did we just fix the problem of being apart or what?" Shane said, smiling at her friends over the video chat. "You two are amazing. We going back to Cali … Cali … Cali." They all began to sing.

She called Nigel next, but he wasn't as easy of a sale. He figured she would leave him and never look back. If anybody should be heading to the West Coast, it was probably him. With the talent he had, he could go anywhere, but he chose to stay in Port City.

That wasn't attractive to Shane. She was an adventure in a bottle, and he was complacent. She felt bad that she was leaving him, but he was too scared to make big moves. If they had been together sooner, she was sure that she could have made him into a better man.

She was tired of hearing him complain about it. "Just come with me, then."

"I can't. I told you. I don't have my paper right yet. When I do, I'm going to L.A. too."

"Um-hm." She didn't believe him. He had been promising to move to L.A. for forever. "Sounds like a bunch of excuses to me, Nigel. You have a ready-made gig."

"You don't understand the life of DJing. It's all about your name, and I don't have a name in L.A."

"You never will if you stay here. It's never going to be perfect. You just have to do it. Just jump."

"Not everyone has Daddy's safety net, Shane."

"Boy, my daddy ain't financing this. I have scholarships and money saved. I'm about my hustle. Don't get it twisted." *Who does he think he is talking to? Do your homework, homeboy.* "Dude, I gotta go. I have to celebrate, and this is not what I had in mind." She hung up before he could say good-bye. It was rude, but it was right. She was over his negativity, over his lack of ambition, over her boy toy.

She got off the phone with Nigel and ran downstairs just in time to watch her father join the FBI agent in his car. She ran outside. "Daddy? Daddy, what's going on?"

"Shane, go back in the house. I'm just helping the agency find Betancourt. That's all."

"Daddy?" She felt that there was more

to the story than he was telling her. She ran in the house to call Marisa. Her father had just been taken in for questioning too. Their day had turned on a dime. They went from celebrating to mourning in minutes.

She waited by the window for hours. She didn't think she would ever see her father again. She was preparing herself for the worst.

"Shane, get away from that window. You've been there for hours. It's not going to bring your father home any sooner."

"Mom, what if he winds up taking the fall for Mister Betancourt? I watch Lifetime movies. I know what could happen."

"Fosters don't lose. Daddy will be fine. Now come on, let's order a movie or something. It'll make the time pass by faster."

Just as they were about to retreat into the living room, they heard his keys in the door. They both sat frozen. *Is it really him? Is it Daddy?* It was. They jumped on him. He looked tired, exhausted even.

He kissed them both. "Baby, will you fix me a plate?"

Her mother retreated into the kitchen, and she watched as her father slumped down into his favorite chair. "What do you think, Daddy? Will they ever catch him?"

"I don't know, but George and I are doing everything we can to help. He can't get away with this, not in Port City."

At least it sounded as though her father wasn't in trouble. She was relieved. She kissed him and ran upstairs to her room. No more than five minutes passed before she was back downstairs and in the kitchen making cookies. She could hear her mother and father whispering. Her mother's voice sounded strained.

"I have some money, but I don't know how long it will sustain us."

"Well, we are going to need it. They froze all of my accounts. They said that it would open up after they completed their investigation."

"Investigations can take a long time."

"I know, but what can we do?"

"I don't understand how this even fell in our lap," her mom said.

"Well, since I introduced him to George, it could be considered a conspiracy."

"That is crazy. Well, who introduced the two of you?" she demanded.

"I met him at—" Just as Shane tried to pull the cookie sheet out, the other pans fell inside the pantry, clanging against one another. "Who's in the kitchen?" her father yelled.

"It's just me. I was making cookies, and—"

"And eavesdropping on our conversation?" her mother asked.

"Oh ... no ... I ..."

"I know when you are lying, Shane Renée. What did you hear?"

"Daddy, I don't want to talk about it. Please, I'm sorry I heard anything. I only wanted some cookies."

"Well, I'll tell you what, don't go out of this house telling our business. I'm serious, Shane. This one's too important."

"Why did they freeze your accounts? Do they think—"

"Hey, listen to me. George and I did nothing wrong. We just can't have people speculating on why the FBI is doing this or that."

The next morning, the FBI's assumptions were the top story in the *Port City Gazette*, so there was no reason to hide anything anymore. This had just turned ugly for the Fosters and the Maldonados.

# CHAPTER 16

## New York, New York

$\mathcal{T}$he girls thought they would be on cloud nine when they arrived in the Big Apple, but their mood was so solemn it was becoming contagious. The situation back in Texas was stressing the whole school out. Other students weren't in the thick of it like Shane and Marisa's parents, but a lot of people were affected directly by the Betancourt scandal or had a friend or family member affected.

With the Foster family and the Maldonado family in the center of the whole
debacle, it was hard to focus on enjoying
their getaway. And after the long bus ride,
the senior class was beginning to grumble.
They wanted to get to New York and kick
back in their cozy hotel rather than go out,
but their sponsors would hear none of it.

Shane went over to Mrs. Monroe. "Mrs.
Monroe?"

"What, Shane?" She never took the
sleeping mask off her face.

"Are you asleep?"

"Not since you woke me up."

"Can we just stay in tonight? I'm not
feeling up to the whole dinner in the city
thing. I'm feeling more like ..."

Mrs. Monroe removed the mask and
looked directly at Shane. "I appreciate all
of the hard work you did getting everybody here, but this is no longer about
you. The entire senior class is here, and I
cannot cater to you. Now sit down while

the bus is moving." She put her mask back on her face, leaving Shane with her mouth wide open.

"How did it go?" Brandi asked, thinking that they would get on Friender and find out where the real New York teens were going to be hanging out. She knew that would lift their spirits, not hanging out with the senior class yet again.

"Not good. She's keeping us under lock and key for now."

When the buses pulled into the parking garage of their hotel, they were impressed. The hotel had the luxury of a large chain, but it was designed for only a few hundred guests. Luckily, they were able to occupy the entire hotel.

Once they were all given their room keys, Mrs. Monroe stood up to give them the plans for the rest of the evening. "Everyone has one hour to freshen up and get back down here. We have dinner reservations, and then we are going on a tour."

Everyone began cheering. "There are a lot of great spots all around us, but we just want to make sure that you know what's here before we start letting you roam around. Remember the buddy system. Always stay with at least one person, and don't leave without them."

She was right. They were just blocks from Broadway and in walking distance of great shopping, eating, and most importantly, the venue for the *Teen Bites* Awards.

After the girls showered and dressed, they went to meet with the rest of the senior class. They took pictures in the lobby of the hotel, and headed out to Wolfgang's Steakhouse. As soon as they walked in, they felt out of place. With white tablecloths and soft music, they felt out of their comfort zones. They were ushered to their private party room, where they could gawk and react the way they wanted to.

"I could swear I just saw Turtle from *Entourage*," someone whispered.

"I thought I saw Tom Cruise's baby mama," someone else whispered.

They were starstruck. Mrs. Monroe, Mrs. Woods, and Mrs. Scapin looked as though they were right at home, even though they were among stars. Shane, Brandi, and Marisa watched as they maneuvered through the tables, catching glances from the men probably making deals worth millions of dollars.

"One thing's for sure, there's something about a Texas woman," Shane said, knowing that she would be like them one day.

"So this is how the other half lives," Brandi said, looking at their dining area.

They started out with a small salad, accompanied by a variety of Wolfgang Puck's own signature dressings labeled in fancy serving dishes on the table. They were each served sparkling apple cider in beautifully crafted champagne flutes. Everything was new for them. Across the room, the attitudes of the seniors were different than just a year ago—more mature, more serene.

The chaperones chatted away at their own table, enjoying a nice break from the teens. They laughed heartily as they monitored their students. They knew they had chosen the right restaurant. This experience was huge for some of the students who never really had an opportunity to venture outside of Port City.

Hannah, Shane, Brandi, Marisa, and Riley sat at one table. Right next to them was the hotheaded football team: Matthew, Jaylon, Mario, and Tyson. They were the reason that Coach Davis had even come on the trip. Matthew had a scholarship to Texas A&M, and Coach Davis was not about to let him blow it.

Jaylon, Mario, and Tyson had spent the end of football season at the alternative campus for the prank they pulled on their rivals at the beginning of the school year.

Their parents were disappointed that with all of their talent, they were overlooked by the major colleges. They couldn't take a chance on boys who would blow their senior year on a prank. Luckily, they were placed at various junior colleges in Texas. If they proved that they could keep their cool, the possibility of them being picked up by a D-1 school was still a possibility.

"Man, I ain't never been in no restaurant like this," Jaylon admitted.

"I don't think any of us have," Matthew joined in. "When my mom and dad were married, these kinds of restaurants were for date night only."

Shane turned around and looked at them. "Why y'all gotta sound country?"

"Said the girl with the Southern drawl," Brandi clowned her. "Girl, we all sound country. We are country compared to these East Coast people. You hear how they talk?"

Marisa sat quietly, taking it all in. She

wanted to carve a piece of this and take it back to Port City with her. New York! It was as though she could touch the magic of the city. The way the people looked and talked. She was falling in love.

To simplify the orders, Mrs. Monroe had a special menu for their group. They chose from three options as the chef came out of the kitchen to greet them. He then lavished them with delicacies from the kitchen.

When the desserts came by, Shane declared, "This is living."

"I love it here," Riley said as she took a bite of crème brûlée. She took a deep breath. She had come so far in her four years at PCH. She had gone from smoking weed and popping pills to being in the top ten percent of her class and holding down a part-time job.

The day she had gone to see Shane in the hospital during ninth grade had been her turning point. She saw the road that Shane had traveled and was determined not to make the same mistakes. Everyone always knew she was a smart girl. And she was still Riley, just a little more cautious.

They walked back to their hotel through the heart of Times Square, drinking in the ambience of the city. "Stay together. Head count as soon as we get to the hotel," Mrs. Monroe told them.

"This is like a dream. Thank you so much, Shane, for making this happen," Marisa whispered, slipping her arm into Shane's.

"You like it here, huh? Better than Arkansas?" She looked deeply into her friend's eyes, as though she could see her soul. "This is where you belong, Mari. I know the look. It was the same one I had when you took me to Cali with you."

Marisa smiled. She had been thinking the same thing. Shane knew her so well. "I know. I'm getting into Julliard. If I don't get in now, I'll get in later."

"I'll hold down the West Coast. You

hold down the East Coast. And Bran can take care of that good ol' Third Coast."

"That's a lot of land in between us."

"I know, but it's who we are. We have to be true to ourselves, and the three of us are so different."

Back at the hotel, Mrs. Monroe took a head count. She told everyone they had a few minutes before the start of the tour.

Out in the city, they found restaurants, shopping locations, museums, everything that was New York. The school had them on a tight schedule. The first round of screenings for *Teen Bites* was set to begin at nine thirty in the morning.

By day three of the trip, the students loved the New York lifestyle. Marisa wasn't the only one drawn to the city. Mrs. Woods even scheduled a tour for a group of students who wanted to visit NYU. Marisa realized that she didn't have to be accepted at Julliard. She could attend NYU!

"There's no way you can get into this school," Riley told her. "Even for an emergency application, it's too late."

Marisa was stoic as she spoke to the counselor that the tour guide introduced them to. She listened intently as the counselor detailed all of the things NYU had to offer. Marisa felt as though she wanted to cry. She wanted New York to be in her future so bad that she could taste it, but tears and New York didn't mix. She was going to have to toughen up if she was going to live in the Big Apple.

"Ma'am, may I speak to you privately?" she asked as the counselor bid farewell to the group.

"Of course."

"I need to attend NYU." She detailed everything that had happened since Hurricane Adam, and how she was left without a college to attend. She left out the part about being accepted at the University of Arkansas and Baymont College. She knew she didn't belong at either. She wanted snow, subways, and Central Park.

"Come to my office." She followed the counselor as she put her at a computer to fill out their online application. "I won't have your records, but I should be able to—"

Marisa reached in her bag, pulling out the necessary paperwork. "Mrs. ..."

"Miss Cruz."

"Miss Cruz, I'm serious. I want this. I am fully prepared." She pulled out a copy of her résumé.

"You are a model? This is quite an impressive résumé, Miss Maldonado. Your grades look good. Your SATs are impressive. How have you not been placed in one of the top schools? I have to make some calls, pull some strings, and talk to some people," she said, laughing. "But I have a way of making things happen. I'll take care of this. What number should I use to contact you?"

Marisa wrote it down quickly and shook her hand before she reached out and hugged Miss Cruz, who was so shocked that she didn't even hug her back. "I'm sorry. We are huggers in Texas."

"Okay," Miss Cruz answered. "I promise. You'll hear from me."

The awards ceremony was scheduled to take place that night. They all quickly put on their best dresses and heels. It was their first red carpet affair, and they had brought the largest group to the event. By the time Marisa met up with her friends, Shane was a ball of nerves.

"There are some really good films out there."

"I know! Did you get to see the one about the kids smoking synthetic weed? It was crazy," Brandi told her.

"No, but I did see the one about the kids making themselves pass out to get high. It was so good. I can't believe that

I'm even here. Do you think I even stand a chance to win?"

"Shane Foster does not doubt herself. You know doggone well that you should be here," Brandi fussed. "Now walk into that awards ceremony like first place is yours. I hope you have a speech ready."

"A speech?" Shane looked bewildered.

They left her alone so that she would have time to think and to breathe. She needed it. Hannah joined her at their table. They had worked hard.

"Did you get to see any of the other documentaries?" Hannah asked her.

"Yeah."

"I thought they were good, but not as good as ours. Did you like them better than *The Blues*?"

"Not at all. I may be biased, though." They began the ceremony with a roar from the crowd.

"Welcome to *Teen Bites*!" the announcer

yelled into the microphone, and the crowd yelled back. This was not an event for the cool kids on the block. These were journalism kids—artsy, creative, different. Nobody looked like they were from Port City. Each group had a different vibe from their own states. It was much different than what the Port City kids were used to.

It was a night of watching clips from the best of the best in the nation, and the PCH section roared when *The Blues* flickered across the screen. It was insane to see their little town on the oversized screen. They watched intently throughout the night as awards were handed out for best docudrama, best short, best mockumentary, and then the most important of all, best documentary of the year.

"This is it," Shane said, holding tightly to Hannah's arm.

They were bouncing in their seats. "Third place goes to ... *I Cut*!" The group from Chicago began celebrating. They were all still in high school and knew the clout this award would bring. Third place was almost as good as winning.

"Second place goes to ... *Sex-Teen Years*!" This group of students was from St. Petersburg, Florida.

"Omigod ... omigod ... We are either all in or all out," Hannah said, grabbing Shane.

"I know. I know."

"First place ... and winner of this year's best *Teen Bites* documentary ... *The Blues*!"

Everyone from Port City went wild. It was like walking in a dream as Shane, Hannah, and the rest of the journalism team went to accept their award. Mrs. Monroe stood on the side of the stage, smiling up at her group. She was so proud.

Shane gave a speech, thanked a bunch of people, and walked back to her table in a daze. If her speech had not been recorded, she would have never remembered what she said or whom she thanked. It was a dream come true.

They left *Teen Bites* with two more days in New York. Shane finally got to sit back and enjoy the trip without the stress of the competition. They even got to go to the day club for teens twenty and under. It was a new experience—music, appetizers, a dance floor. The windows were painted black so it looked like an actual club. They were dancing and enjoying just being girls let loose in the big city.

Shane headed to the bar for a bottle of water. She felt a hand on the small of her back and turned around quickly. It was Dustin Chaisson. "Hey, I just wanted to congratulate you. I always knew you were an awesome girl."

"You are pretty awesome yourself, Dustin." She liked him. Their situation was just wrong place, wrong time. "I just wish ..."

He shook his head. "Don't. Let's just

leave it at that." He kissed her on the fore-head and went back over to his boys.

"Miss, your water," the bartender said, trying to get her attention.

"Oh, yeah, thanks."

She could see Brandi and Marisa on the dance floor. They were having fun. "Thank you, God," she said, basking in the moment. In New York, in this moment, they were free.

# CHAPTER 17

# Recovered

*I*t was time to say good-bye to the East Coast, Broadway, and New York City. It was time to get back to Port City—back to the problems that went along with being who they were. The girls were wrapped up in their blankets, ready for the long trip of movies, books, and card games. Everybody had a tablet of some sort close to them. But traveling by bus was still a long haul.

Hours into the trip, there was a picture of Mr. Foster in handcuffs. Shane could tell one of their neighbors had snapped the picture. She was in shock. He was being tried right there on Friender. People didn't even have the facts. Later there were more pictures. This time it was Mr. Maldonado.

"Why is this bus taking so long?" Marisa asked impatiently. "It didn't take us this long to get to New York."

"Girl, this is a bus. Not a Learjet. It did take this long. You're just stressed. Send me a game. That'll take your mind off what's going on," Brandi said.

"Count me out," Shane told them, gazing out the window. She was texting Robin, trying to get a play-by-play of what was going on at home.

Robin didn't know anything. They hadn't seen or heard from Mr. Foster since the FBI showed up earlier that morning. Friender was going nuts with mean comments. There was no way to tell what was true or false. Shane knew the only way to make sense of it was to talk to her dad. But that didn't seem likely any time soon.

When they finally were able to stop,

stretch their legs, and get a bite to eat, Marisa received a text from Nadia that read, "Papa is home! Shhh!"

"Shhh?" she responded.

Marisa read it and she reread it. *Why is it a secret that Papa's home? Who would even care?* Her thoughts were broken as Shane plopped down in the seat beside her as she received another text from Nadia. "Mr. Foster ... *no bueno*," it read.

"I can't believe what's happening to our fathers. I need chocolate to get me through this one," Shane said, tearing open her Snickers. She rambled on and on about how they were in this together and their fathers were innocent. She just knew it ... Blah, blah, blah.

"Papa is at home, Shane," Marisa blurted out. "He's at home."

"Well then, that means that—"

"No, Shane. I don't think it means what you want it to mean."

She had tried to keep quiet like Nadia

had said, but she couldn't let her girl go on like that. Shane was thinking *right*, and life was going *left*. She had to prepare her for the truth. Whatever was happening, things were moving fast, and they were approaching Port City within hours.

"But—"

"The line for the restroom was horrible," Brandi said, joining her friends across the aisle. "What'd I miss?"

Shane jumped up and ran off the bus. She needed fresh air. *They're going to make him take the fall for this. It was all a set-up!* She could see Betancourt's face as he ate their food, laughed in their faces, and plotted to take everything from them. Or did her father have enemies who would go this far? There was no way to know. The list of people who disliked politicians was a mile long.

"Shane," Dustin said, startling her. "You okay?"

"You scared me, Dustin."

"Hey, you are going to be okay."

"You have no idea."

"I have eyes, and I do know how to read," he said. "It's all over Friender."

"Yeah, I guess there are no secrets anymore, huh?"

"I'm going to get you some water. Pull yourself together. What's the worst that can happen?" he asked.

"My father could take the fall for stealing all of the FEMA money, get kicked off of the city council, do time in jail, and be separated from his family for years for something he did not do."

"Nah, not gonna happen," Dustin proclaimed.

"How do you know that? Look, I need to make a call. I'll meet you on the bus." She called her big sister. She knew Robin would give it to her straight.

"Shane?" Her sister sounded panicked. "How much longer will it be before you get home?"

"It's hard to say."

"Okay, I'll have to talk to you when you get home ... the phone lines are ... compromised."

*Compromised? What are we dealing with here?* "Oh-kay ..." She didn't know what to think. That was like a conversation from a TV show or something, not one you had in real life.

Hours later, the bus pulled up at PCH. Shane endured the looks from her fellow students as they half-heartedly congratulated her on her victory. Most avoided her like the plague. They had either gossiped too much or felt embarrassed for her. Either way, it had been a long trip, and they all wanted to get away from each other.

Shane sped home, trying to get answers from her mother and sister. When she walked in the door, she saw her father sitting at the kitchen table talking to the agents. He quickly rushed over to Shane, who was in tears.

"Daddy, they said that ..."

"Don't worry, my sweet girl. How did you get past security?"

"Into my own house? Come on, Dad." Her father should have known her better. She could talk her way in anywhere. "Now, tell me what's going on. Your walk of shame is all over the Internet. You're supposed to be in jail."

"Exactly, and that's what you are supposed to think too. Now, a car is going to take you to the Haywood's home. We are closing in on Betancourt. This phony arrest is what's going to do it. Trust me?"

"Of course." An agent escorted her to the Haywood home. She was sworn to secrecy. If she talked, it would blow the whole investigation.

Brandi was almost asleep when Shane crept into her room. "How's the fam?" she asked groggily.

"Go back to sleep. We'll talk about it tomorrow," Shane whispered.

By the morning, news broke that Mr. Betancourt was arrested. The FEMA money had been recovered. It was the greatest moment of Shane's life.

Mr. Maldonado's construction business was also cleared of wrongdoing. They were back in business. With their bank accounts unfrozen, they could finally repair the homes of their friends, family, and neighbors. It was a good day, and a time of restoration.

# CHAPTER 18

# *Marisa*

The girls' senior year had been one of turmoil mixed in with wonderful memories. It was just their life: drama, followed by calm. The long bus ride had taken its toll on all of them. It was as if they needed a break from spring break, but there were only two days left, not enough time to fully recuperate.

Ashley Rivera called Marisa on video chat. "Congrats on the whole conspiracy thing," Ashley said half-heartedly.

"Thanks, Ashley," Marisa responded dryly. This was the last thing she wanted to be doing right now, having a conversation with Ashley. Soon, she would just be a memory in Marisa's life, nothing more. After a long silence, Marisa asked, "Why are you really calling me, Ashley?"

"I don't want you to think that there was anything going on with Trent and me."

"I don't even care, Ashley."

"I'm sure you do," Ashley asserted.

"Then why go out there and holler at him if you thought that I cared?" Marisa asked.

"It was innocent enough. Arkansas offered me a full scholarship. Trent's the only person I know there. What would you have done?"

"I don't know," she said, turning on her. "There are a lot of things that you did that I wouldn't have done, so I can't answer that. We are way different from each other, Ashley. I'm not saying that one is better than the other, just different."

"Well, I wanted you to hear it from me.

I'm going to Arkansas, and it has nothing to do with Trent."

"Whatever, Ashley. Is that it? Is that your big revelation?"

"I just wanted to ... I don't know."

"Look, this call wasn't for me. It was for you. Do you feel better now?" Marisa asked.

"Hey, I'm not asking you to trust me, but trust Trent. Don't give up your relationship for something that didn't even happen, 'cause nothing happened."

"Ashley, there's so much you don't know about my relationship with Trent. You are not the reason that I'm not going to be with him. Trent is."

"Good."

They ended their conversation where they always did, full of doubt and uncertain of what to believe.

"Don't believe anything ashy Ashley says," Shane warned her after they hung up.

"Yeah, I don't trust all that either. And why is she calling you?" Brandi asked.

"There's no need to discuss it. They are both irrelevant at this point," Marissa declared.

Marisa had been in turmoil since returning from New York. She was dying for a call from Miss Cruz at NYU. She knew if she didn't get the call, she could possibly wind up with Trent and Ashley in Arkansas. That would be like taking two steps in the wrong direction. She wanted to move forward, not backward. It was time to grow up. She didn't want to bring their childishness into her new life.

The day Miss Cruz finally called her phone, NYU was the furthest thing from her mind. She had been on the phone with Marcie Miller. When talking business, she never even looked at her other line. She had a photo shoot coming up. That's where her attention was focused. When she hung up, she had almost forgotten about the other call.

She looked down at her phone in amazement. She had a voice mail waiting. Then she saw the 212 area code. Her stomach began to flip. She pressed Play.

"Hello, this is Miss Cruz from NYU. I'm calling for Marisa Maldonado. Marisa, please give me a call at your earliest convenience." She pressed the Call Back button before she could even allow her brain the time to process.

"Hello, Miss Cruz? This is Marisa Maldonado."

"Marisa, how are you today? I'm so sorry that it took me so long to get back to you ..." She started to give reasons for the delay, but Marisa had long ago tuned her out. She was waiting to hear the phrase, the one that would change her life: you are in.

"Miss Cruz, is there any news about my acceptance at NYU?"

"Oh, yes ... I'm sorry." Marisa's heart

dropped when she heard those words. It was exactly what she didn't want to hear. Miss Cruz continued, "That's why I called. You are in! We would love to have you at NYU this fall."

Marisa's hand went to her mouth, as if that alone would block her scream from escaping. Tears fell as she allowed the words to sink in. Miss Cruz chattered away, like her words weren't life-changing. Marisa shook her head in disbelief. She started to take notes. Miss Cruz needed more paperwork. There were financial applications to submit. Miss Cruz would document everything in an e-mail. Good thing since Marisa's head was exploding with joy.

As soon as she pressed End on the phone, she began to scream. She sang the song that would be the soundtrack of her new life. "New York, New York! If I can make it there, I'll make it anywhere. I'm goin' to New York!"

Her mother stood at her door. "Mi hija, what did you say?" her mother asked, putting her dishrag into her apron before reaching out for her daughter.

"I did it!" she screamed. "I'm going to NYU!"

## CHAPTER 19

# Shane

Graduation was around the corner. But preparing for the next phase of life hadn't really hit the girls yet.

Shane walked into the kitchen to join her mother as she prepared Saturday morning breakfast. She never heard her until Shane opened the refrigerator door. Kim Foster turned around to see who had intruded on her moment of Zen.

"Mom, why are you crying? Where's Daddy? What's wrong?"

"Nothing, my baby. Nothing's wrong." She held tightly to a picture in her hand.

"Why are you holding this?" She took the familiar baby picture from her mom's hand. It was Shane smiling widely in her pink and black birthday dress.

"Your first birthday. My baby's leaving me," her mother sobbed. "I don't want to make you sad, but I hate to see you go."

"Oh, Mom. I'll never leave you. No matter how many miles separate us, I'll never leave you. Stop crying or you'll make me cry too!"

Her mother hugged her tightly. Mrs. Foster pulled her daughter away and looked at her intently. She nodded her approval and handed her an envelope. Shane opened the letter from UCLA.

She was sure it was a retraction. The acceptance letter had been a mistake. But no. They were inviting her to join them for their summer program. She had to report to Los Angeles the first week of July. Her win at *Teen Bites* had prompted them to open a spot for her. The summer program was for the brightest and most promising film students.

"Mommy, did you read this?"

"I confess I did. Congratulations, my love." She kissed her daughter again. "You have already exceeded my dreams for you. Everyone is going to be so disappointed that you have to leave a month early, but you can't miss this opportunity."

"I know."

"So we are all going to take a family vacation to L.A. over the Independence holiday, and then I will go to UCLA with you and help get your dorm room set up."

"Mom, we can't fly the whole family to L.A. for me! I can manage on my own."

"Well, that's one worry you won't have because I'll be right there by your side. No way is my baby starting school and taking care of all of that on her own. No way."

"Thanks, Mom!"

Shane couldn't even eat breakfast. She was so excited. She called Nigel and made nice. He had all the hookups in Port City, and she was ready to celebrate. He had a gig that night at the Room. She called her girls and prepared them for the evening ahead.

"I can't go out tonight, Shane. I'm going to Austin for my last debate next weekend. I have to prepare," Brandi said.

"B, you can be too focused. Don't worry about it. You are a natural, and you are going to do great. Come let all that pretty hair down and get the Room turned up. Port City needs us."

"They need us?" Marisa asked, laughing. "B, this is one debate you may lose. I mean, Port City *needs* us. How can you say no to that?"

And they didn't say no. They hit the stage as soon as they got to the Room. They took the mic from DJ Dazed, and that was that. Inhibitions went out the window as they partied with all their friends. The senior class was in the building.

DJ Dazed took the mic from Shane just as she was about to do another shout out to the PCH senior class. "We have a VIP just walking into the spot. Lil Flo is in the building."

Lil Flo had her whole entourage with her and a string of guys following her every move.

"Yo, my bad," DJ Dazed continued. "My boy in the building. He needs no introduction. Give it up for Young Dub!"

Dub hit the stage two steps at a time. "Yoooo!" He was slurring and staggering as he performed his latest hit. Nobody was in a seat or standing against a wall. They were all rapping, as if they had coauthored the song themselves. It was time to turn up Texas style, and Third Coast Records was making sure this was the case.

Dub left the stage, red cup in hand, on a mission to find Brandi.

"Shane!" he yelled, giving her a big hug. "Where B at?"

"Dude, you on one tonight. She's right there. I gotta roll, Dub."

"Yo, Beaty looking for you and Mari. Don't play him to the left."

"When have I ever played Beaty to the left?" He was Dub's producer and Shane's favorite person. She moved out of the way. Brandi was standing right behind her.

"There, baby, go."

"You're messed up, Dub. Dang, what you been doing?" Brandi asked.

"I've been doing me, especially since my number one leaving me."

"Don't you dare blame me," Brandi snapped.

Lil Flo was onstage doing her latest girls anthem as the females surrounded the stage. She was in her zone.

"And you showed up with Flo? You took her to our crib too?" Brandi hissed. "You couldn't have thought that I'd come running into your arms with her here."

"Man, Third Coast Records paid for the

limo. I ain't checkin' for Flo, and she ain't checkin' for me. Just relax, mami. I came here for you." He grabbed her and didn't let go. It was familiar and fun. All females were looking at her as she cozied up with Port City's finest. They had no idea the drama he had put her through.

Shane, Beaty, and Marisa joined them as the crowd began chanting for more Young Dub. They wanted to hear some of his throwback cuts, and he was quick to oblige.

"What's up with yo boy?" Shane asked Beaty as they watched Dub stagger through the crowd.

"He's an artist. You know how they roll."

"It don't make it cute. I know turnt up. That used to be me."

"I heard. By the time you started rolling with us, that was over," Beaty said.

"Yeah, well, I'm worried about my boy," Shane confessed.

Dub was in full groove and so was the crowd. Just as he raised his cup and was about to exit the stage, he fell to the floor. Young Dub passed out at the end of his performance. Shane's journalism team was there, cameras in tow. She tried to get them to put the cameras down.

Shane felt as though she was chasing camera flashes, but it was easier than chasing down the pictures later. Anybody worth their salt in journalism would have wanted to document this event, but that was *her* boy. She wasn't going to have him all over Friender looking jacked up.

Brandi and Beaty were next to him on the stage as Marisa frantically dialed 911. Shane watched from a distance as the owners of the Room tried to clear the place out. She could hear an ambulance in the distance. She was so happy they had been there. She couldn't imagine hearing about this while in her pajamas at home. Brandi would have never forgiven herself. They were right where they needed to be, by Young Dub's side.

# CHAPTER 20

# Brandi

$B$y the time Brandi returned home from school, the contractors were cleaning up as they completed the final touches on her family's home. It looked like a new place. New floors, new paint, new carpet, new windows, and a sturdy roof.

It had been a long time since they had no worries when the weatherman announced a chance of rain. When the FEMA money was returned, Mr. Maldonado made sure that their home was the first one completed with the highest-quality construction materials. He even threw in extras. As promised, he had taken care of his long-time friends.

They sat down for dinner. Catherine Haywood insisted on one family meal a day. It was sacred. She served up pork chops, garlic mashed potatoes, and fresh green beans picked from their garden.

"Brandi, how is your rapper friend? Is he doing better?" her mother asked.

"I think so, Mom. He's in a rehab facility now." She avoided her father's gaze as he looked at her. The last thing he wanted for his daughter was to be caught up in a world of drugs and addiction.

"Well, you can't leave for Austin too soon for me. It's time for you to get away from Port City," he said to her. "Now, this competition of yours, what time do we need to be on the road?"

"We really should leave first thing in the morning," her mother said. She had every detail of their trip already mapped out. "Do you think you are ready, Bran?"

"She's ready, Mom. Brandi's always ready," Raven said with a mouthful of mashed potatoes. "I can't wait to see you up on that stage."

"Next time, sing my praises after you are done chewing. That's just nasty, RaRa."

After dinner, they loaded up the truck so that they wouldn't be running around like crazies in the morning.

After a good night's sleep, they took the long drive to Austin. In the car, Brandi sent Erick a text message letting him know when she would be arriving and her hotel arrangements. When she arrived, there were a dozen white roses waiting at the front desk for her. She read the card, "You are going to do great. Love, E."

"Who are they from, Bran?" Raven asked, trying to sneak a peek at the card.

"They're from Erick."

"I like that boy," her mother and father said in unison.

"I do too," she admitted to them.

After getting settled at the hotel, Brandi met up with her team to iron out some of the details of the debate. They had been sent possible topics a few weeks back. They had researched as much as humanly possible. Now they were ready.

The next day, they arrived at the capitol building where the debate was to take place. It was massive, beautiful, and historic all wrapped up in one. They could feel the energy in the air. They were greeted by the Speaker of the Texas House of Representatives. The students were a bit starstruck. He told them that he too had been a member of the debate team and had won the year he competed.

"This weekend is one that you won't forget for a long time," he said. "Enjoy yourselves and have a great time."

The PCH team was escorted to their preparation area. There, Mr. McAfee addressed them. "I know you can do this.

Don't let the location change who you are. Fear no man but God, and show this team from San Angelo what you are made of in Port City. I chose you four for this debate because you are the best. Now go out there and prove to them what I already know. Hands in."

They made a circle and put their hands in the center. "Pooooort City!" they yelled, making a thumbs-up motion in unison.

Brandi stood up when it was her turn. She could feel all eyes on her as she went up to make the closing remarks. She could see her family, Erick, and the UT recruiter. They were all there. She knew that a victory rested on her shoulders. The topic was welfare reform.

She wanted to be true to the people who she knew relied on government assistance. She opened her mouth to speak and the words died in her throat. She didn't know if she could recover. She looked down at her notes. They weren't right. They weren't what she was feeling at that moment. She closed her eyes and began to speak.

"My family went through a difficult time this year as we tried to pick up the pieces after Hurricane Adam took everything from us. There seemed to be nowhere to turn, nobody to help us. FEMA, which is a government run program, was there for us. We just needed a little help during a time when everyone had so little. That's what some of the families in America are going through today."

She gazed out at the audience, more confident in her words. "We can't possibly turn our backs on those families as my opponents suggest. Ending welfare is not the solution to our country's problems. There does need to be a system in place for those people living on welfare for too long. We have let those people down," Brandi said. "We can only be judged by how we treat those in our country in need of the most help. As my team stated earlier, we have to educate those on assistance so that they can stand on their own. Whatever we do, we cannot turn our backs on them."

Her voice grew stronger and more confident with each word. "I stand before you today as a living witness that sometimes you need a little help to point your family in the right direction. So, no, we are not in a position to end welfare. We *are* in a position to make a change in the United States that will enable families for generations to come. We have to send the message: we have your back, even when it's up against the wall."

Her family stood up and clapped at her final words. The rest of the crowd followed suit. The judges conferred. It was a PCH victory.

As the leader of her team, the Speaker presented the trophy to Brandi. Cameras flashed in every direction as the Port City debate team surrounded her, holding their trophy in the air. It was a sweet victory.

She joined Erick as he wrapped her in his arms. "I knew that you would knock it out of the park. You were amazing."

Mr. McAfee was happy to see Erick there. He had been one of the best debaters that Mr. McAfee had ever coached. He patted him on the back and turned to Brandi. "You spoke from your heart. It was risky abandoning your notes, but the audience connected with you. Great instincts out there."

"Thanks, Mister McAfee. That means so much to me."

Brandi's family had been waiting close-by for a moment to talk to her. "I am so proud of you," her mother said. "My little girl ... quite the woman now."

"We can't wait to officially welcome you to UT this fall. You did a great job, Brandi," the UT recruiter said, shaking her hand. "I wish that I could join you for dinner, but I have to run."

"No problem. Thanks so much for coming. I'm so excited about coming to Austin," Brandi said, glowing in her victory.

Her father grabbed her and rubbed the top of her head. She hated when he did that. He always messed up her hair. Today, she didn't complain. It was his way of showing his love.

They went out to eat and enjoyed a little bit of the Austin nightlife. Erick was a great tour guide, taking them to the legendary Stubb's Barbeque House, where live music was playing.

"Omigod, this is so good," Brandi said as she bit into the jalapeño-flavored roast beef.

"Spectacular," her mother agreed.

Erick took Brandi closer to the band and away from her family. They listened to the music for a while until Erick turned to her. "Don't feel like you have to be with me when you come to UT. I know that you want to experience college life."

"E, I can't even imagine what my life here would be like without you. Let's just let it flow naturally, no expectations. Is that okay with you?"

"It's better than okay."

The Haywood family packed up the next morning, sad that their mini-vacation had come to an end. "This was the greatest weekend ever," Brandi said, putting the last suitcase in the truck.

"It was," her mother agreed. "Now the next time we see Austin, we will be dropping you off to stay. How do you feel about that?"

"I can't wait, Mom."

"I can," Raven said, imagining her life without her sister. "I don't want you to be this far away. Do you have to leave, Bran?"

"I do and someday you do too. And when that day comes, I'll be right by your side. No matter how many miles separate us. I'll always be a phone call away. If it gets too hard on you, I'll be there. I promise. I've taken care of you from the moment Mommy and Daddy brought you home from the hospital, and I always will."

Raven hugged her sister tightly. She knew that if Brandi said it, then that's the way it would be. Her big sister never let her down.

# CHAPTER 21

# To New Beginnings

They stood in the mirror at Brandi's newly renovated house in their blue caps and gowns, admiring their reflections. They were here. It was time. What mixed feelings, closing the chapter on high school.

"It seems like we just started school. Now it's over," Marisa said on the verge of tears.

"Right?" Brandi chimed in. "Now this is it."

"I'm going to miss y'all, but I'm ready to go," Shane told them.

"I think I am too," Brandi said unapologetically.

"Me too," Marisa said, looking at her friends.

They stood in a circle and prayed together. They prayed for their future, prayed for guidance, prayed for wisdom, and prayed for their families. They knew they would never find friends like this anywhere else. Who could live up to this?

It had been their destiny to be on this journey together. It had been a long road, but God had helped them through it all. They learned that to truly appreciate the good times, bad times had to be sprinkled in. It was just the way it was.

A horn blew outside, and they all ran to the window. There was a limousine parked in the driveway. They ran down the stairs.

"Mom, I can't believe you got me a limo!" Brandi screamed.

"I didn't," her mother said, peeking outside.

Her father was at the front door in a matter of seconds. Before they could ask another question, Young Dub was poking out of the limo's sunroof with a dozen silver-dipped roses to match the tassel hanging from Brandi's graduation cap.

She stopped when she saw him. "Dub, you did this? I didn't even know you were home."

"My boy!" Shane yelled, jumping in the limo with Marisa following closely behind.

Brandi went back to the door where her father stood. "Daddy? Is it okay?"

He smoothed the hair from her face as the wind blew it over her eyes. "Do you think you'll be okay?" he asked, putting the ball in her court. She nodded. "Then it's okay. You are about to be on your own in a few months. I trust you."

She kissed her father and ran to the limo to join her friends. She waved to her mom and Raven, who were watching through the kitchen window.

Dub had champagne flutes and their favorite sparkling apple cider. He filled his own champagne flute with sparkling wine. Brandi tucked herself under his arm. "Thank you so much," she said, looking up at him.

"It's nothing. You deserve it."

They pulled up at the civic center as the senior class was lining up. All heads turned as the limousine crept slowly forward. Shane and Marisa got out, but Dub asked Brandi if he could speak with her for a second.

"B, you know I love you like I've never loved anybody. Sometimes I think I love you more than my own mama."

"No you don't, Dub."

"Yes I do. I know I have a jacked up way of showing it, but yo boy have his own demons that he's wrestling with."

"I know, Dub. I just wish I could be there for you," Brandi said.

"That's kinda what I had in mind." He pulled an envelope out. "Will you go on tour with me?" he asked as a huge smile crept across his face. She opened the envelope. There was a first class ticket to London.

"Oh, Dub." She hugged him tightly. He was *that* guy. The one you knew was so wrong but felt right in the moment. She felt overwhelmed. "Can we talk about it after graduation? I need time to wrap my head around all this."

"Take as much time as you need. Just be at the airport when that plane takes off," he said, laughing.

Brandi got out of the limo and joined her friends in the line. She was confused and torn. She could see Erick in her head. It was like she was in love with two people. When she was with Dub, she was in love with him. When she was with Erick, she was in love with him. She wished she could make up her mind.

"You okay?" Marisa asked.

Brandi nodded and searched the crowd for Shane, who gave her a thumbs-up. She returned the thumbs-up, knowing that they would have a lot to talk about when the ceremony was over.

Four years of school led up to a two-hour ceremony filled with a lot of boring speakers and a lot of picture-taking. By the end, they were all fried. Pictures were hitting Friender before they could even leave the parking lot. They decided to go for all-you-can-eat barbeque crabs. The Maldonados, the Fosters, and the Haywoods were all together.

Brandi, Shane, and Marisa sat together. Brandi pulled out the plane ticket to London and passed it to her two best friends. They looked at each other. "I need to go to the restroom," Shane announced.

"I'm coming too," Marisa said.

Brandi just sat there, and Shane hit her chair. "Oh, me too," Brandi said.

When they got to the restroom, Shane began speaking first. "Look, I love Dub. Love! But you can't go on tour."

"Shane, would *you* pass up this opportunity to go to London?"

"No, but you are not me. You are you," Shane responded.

"You can't go, B," Marisa joined in. "Dub isn't right, not now. Just a month ago we were picking him up off the floor."

"But he went to rehab," Brandi said.

"Unless you want to be in rehab one day, you need to stay in Port City and get ready for college, for UT—"

"For Erick," Marisa completed Shane's sentence.

Brandi looked from friend to friend. "I know, but I feel like he needs me."

"You can't save someone who's drowning. He'll drown you too. Do you want to be your mother?" Shane asked her, forcing her to face a brutal truth.

"No, but ..."

"Then don't go. I know it's looking glamorous now, but I have a bad feeling about this one," Marisa warned her.

"Okay, okay, I won't go."

That was the end of that.


Brandi never looked back. She never wanted to. She was the first to leave Port City, opting to begin her studies at UT during the summer instead of waiting for the fall semester to begin. She had to leave before she made the wrong decision.

She was a phone call away from going to London with Dub, so she just ran. She jumped right in and completed some of her basics before the rest of the newly recruited freshman class even reported to the campus.

Shane had been next. She left for the summer program at UCLA in July. She thought she would have been sad when the day arrived, but she wasn't. There was a new excitement in her that she couldn't hide as she boarded the plane with her family. She was going back to Cali.

Marisa sat patiently in Port City alone, getting her mind and body ready for New York. Her days were filled with yoga and dancing, practice and work. She refused to take calls from Trent. He was bad for her. Marcie Miller was accompanying her to New York to help her get settled.

Marci had a few things she needed to do to ensure that Marisa was making money while in school at NYU. New York was the big time for Marisa and for Marcie too. This was a whole new league for the two of them. It was exciting, intimidating, and refreshing.

"I'm so happy you let me come with you, Marisa. A lot of girls would have opted out of a Houston agency and traded up."

"You were there for me, and I'm staying with you. It's what I'm supposed to do," Marisa said confidently.

"You're one of a kind, Marisa Maldonado."

"Thanks, Marcie Miller. You're not so bad yourself."

The day that Marcie left New York, Marisa knew she was on her own. She enjoyed the big city life. But the sound of a key in her dorm room door startled her back to reality. A girl stood before her with a personality you could almost touch. "I'm Sunshine," she said, dragging in her Louis Vuitton trunks. "I'm your new roommate."

Marisa liked her immediately. She didn't know her story, but she was willing to find out. That night, they stayed up talking and getting to know each other before venturing out to grab a slice of pizza, both excited to conquer new lands.

# Fifteen Years Later

*B*randi watched the television in disbelief as the news unfolded.

Rap phenomenon Young Dub was involved in a single car crash today leaving Staples Center in Los Angeles, where he and long list of stars were performing to raise money for typhoon victims. Dub left Staples Center with an unidentified female companion after his performance.

The rest seemed to be a blur as Brandi collapsed on a sofa in her Austin home. She sat quietly crying as her three-year-old stood by her side. "Why you crying, Mama?"

"Mommy's fine. Go get Daddy," she said to the curly haired little girl, who looked more like her daddy than her mommy.

Erick came running into the living room in his suit, ready to go to court. He had a one thirty appearance and was already late to the office. "What's wrong, Bran? Autumn is freaking out. What happened?" He joined her as she replayed the news on the television.

"I'm so sorry," he said, holding his wife in his arms as she cried. She pulled herself together as Erick wiped away her tears. "Are you going to be okay?" he asked. She nodded her head and kissed him as he left.

"Be careful, my love," she said to Erick before calling for their nanny to take Autumn. She had to call Shane and Marisa.

"Mari, did you hear?"

"I don't hear anything if it doesn't concern one of my models." She had joined Marcie Miller and opened a new modeling agency: Miller and Maldonado Modeling. She ran the New York office while Marcie stayed at the Houston office.

"Dub is gone. He died today in L.A."

"Oh, Bran. I'll be on the next flight out. Call Shane."

Shane was on set. She was always hard to reach. When Isi, Marisa's little sister, had an idea for a new reality show called *L.A. Life*, Shane jumped on it. Isi was a talent unto herself, and if she said that something was hot, it was. The number of followers she had could crash a server.

They were able to locate Shane as she ducked away to video chat with her friends. "What up, BFFs?" she asked happily.

"What's wrong?" Her voice changed when she saw their faces.

"Shane, it's Dub. He's dead." Brandi just ripped the Band-Aid off.

"Again? Girl, they always saying Dub is dead," she quipped.

"It's all over the news: CNN, Inside Edition, local channels."

"I just had lunch with Dub yesterday. He was getting ready for the concert at Staples Center."

Brandi turned her phone to face the television so that Shane could see it for herself.

"I'm on my way to Texas," Shane said. "Isi's coming with me. We are going to have to bring the *L.A. Life* to Port City."

"Are you sure?" Marisa asked, knowing that Isi coming home would mean even more of a media frenzy. "Shane, she'll over-shadow Dub, and this is about him."

"Girl, in Port City can't nobody

overshadow Dub. You all right, Bran? How are you holding?"

"How was he, Shane? When y'all had lunch? Did he ask about me?" Brandi asked. She needed to know.

"He was good, B. He understood why you never called. He respected your decision. That's why he never reached out. He loved you even more for making that choice. He realized you were better off with Erick. And he was so proud of you. Proud of your degree from UT. Then your law degree. He teared up when I showed him pictures of Autumn on Instagram."

"God," Brandi sighed. "I feel so terrible. What about the drugs?"

"Stop. Don't feel terrible. He was incredibly loyal to you. But I think he would have sent you on your way if you had gone to London. Eventually. And the drugs? He was an addict, Bran. You made the right decision with your life. You know what being an addict means. Every day was a struggle for him not to use. That was going to be the focus of a show he pitched to me at lunch. He wanted to be an inspiration to the kids growing up today."

"He will be," Marisa said.

"I'll make sure of it," Shane told them.

The funeral had been a coming home for Port City's finest. The civic center could barely hold all the people who came to celebrate Young Dub's life. The list of names in the audience was impressive. All the rappers from Third Coast, including Lil Flo and the producer, Beaty. Isi Maldonado, who was now a household name. Trent, who had gone pro and was playing for New York. Trent's wife, Ashley, who had her own show on the new Housewife Channel called *DIY with Ashley Walker*. Matthew Kincade, who played for the Atlanta Falcons. And many more.

So many famous names from one small town. It was striking. Port City was a talent breeding ground, and it was more evident today than ever before. They were living proof that it didn't matter where you were from. With drive and determination, you could be whatever you wanted.

As Beaty stood up to eulogize Dub, he talked about the man behind the music. He talked about Devin. Raven held tightly to Autumn. Autumn was Raven's favorite person in the whole world. Since they were in town from Austin, she had spoiled her niece more than any child should be spoiled.

When Beaty started to talk about the one true love of Dub's life, Raven reached out and grabbed her sister's hand. Brandi hadn't talked to him since graduation day. When she didn't show up at the airport, she had made a choice. Erick was her man. Rock steady. She vowed she would never betray him by talking to Dub, and she hadn't. She knew she had done the right thing.

After the funeral, the VIPs went to the museum where they were creating an exhibit in Dub's honor. The mood quickly turned festive as Young Dub's earliest and latest music was played. They dined on shrimp tacos that they all grew up on, bowls of gumbo, and signature lattes. Everybody was still the same. A little more money, a little more experience, and a lot more love.

Ashley and Marisa had learned to coexist, even though Ashley had married Trent.

Ashton sat close to Shane. "When you gonna put me in one of those shows of yours? You know I'm good TV, girl."

"The world is not ready for you, Ashton."

"But maybe it's ready for us." He still knew what to do to make her smile.

"You are still crazy, boy," Shane said.

"Crazy for you."

"Boy, quit!" she said, laughing. Those L.A. guys just did not give her what she needed. They were too pretty. Ashton knew the way to her heart. He was still cute, still funny, and still all about Shane.

They all ended the evening at the Maldonados' new house. It was big enough for all the grandchildren that Nadia and Romero had given them. Autumn was happy to have "cousins" to play with. The Foster family and the Haywood family joined them.

It felt like a homecoming. This was the first time they were all back in Port City at the same time, and they vowed that it wouldn't be the last.

**ABOUT THE AUTHOR**

## Shannon Freeman

$\mathcal{B}$orn and raised in Port Arthur, Texas, Shannon Freeman works full time as an English teacher in her hometown. After completing college at Oral Roberts University, Freeman began her work in the classroom teaching English and oral communications. At that time, the characters of her breakout series, Port City High, began to form, but these characters would not come to life for years. An apartment fire destroyed almost all of the young teacher's worldly possessions before she could begin writing. With nothing to lose, Freeman packed up and headed to Los Angeles, California, to pursue a passion that burned within her since her youth, the entertainment industry.

Beginning in 2001, Freeman made numerous television appearances and enjoyed a rich life full of friends and hard work. In 2008, her world once again changed when she and her husband, Derrick Freeman, found out that they were expecting their first child. Freeman then made the difficult decision to return to Port Arthur and start the family that she had always wanted.

At that time, Freeman returned to the classroom, but entertaining others was still a desire that could not be quenched. Being in the classroom again inspired her to tell the story of Marisa, Shane, and

Brandi that had been evolving for almost a decade. She began to write and the Port City High series was born.

Port City High is the culmination of Freeman's life experiences, including her travels across the United States and Europe. Her stories reflect the friendships she's made across the globe. Port City High is the next breakout series for today's young adult readers. Freeman says, "The topics are relevant and life changing. I just hope that people are touched by my characters' stories as much as I am."